Issue 13 Autumn 2018

Science fiction magazine from Scotland

ISSN 2059-2590
ISBN 978-1-9997002-8-7

Shoreline of Infinity is available in digital or print editions.
Submissions of fiction, art, reviews, poetry, non-fiction are welcomed:
visit the website to find out how to submit.

www.shorelineofinfinity.com

Publisher
Shoreline of Infinity Publications / The New Curiosity Shop
Edinburgh
Scotland

180918

Cover: Siobhan McDonald

Contents

Editorial Team

Co-founder, Editor & Editor-in-Chief:
Noel Chidwick

Co-founder, Art Director:
Mark Toner

Deputy Editor & Poetry Editor:
Russell Jones

Reviews Editor:
Samantha Dolan

Assistant Editor & First Reader:
Monica Burns

Copy editors:
Iain Maloney, Russell Jones, Monica
Burns, Pippa Goldschmidt

Extra thanks to:
Jack Deighton, M Luke McDonell,
Katy Lennon, and many others.

First Contact

www.shorelineofinfinity.com

contact@shorelineofInfinity.com

Twitter: @shoreinf

and on Facebook

We are grateful to **Martyn Turner**,
who sponsored the artwork for *The
Time Between Time* in this issue.
Martyn has supported us on Patreon
for almost two years now and we
thank him for his generosity. For
more information on sponsorship
please visit our Patreon site at
www.patreon.com/shorelineofinfinity

Pull Up a Log

Noel Chidwick

In the last scenes of the film *Cloud Atlas*, Tom Hanks' character is telling his story to his grandchildren around a wood fire set in a circle of stones. In the night sky a pair of moons shine on the calm sea, and his granddaughter asks him to point out distant Earth in amongst the stars. It's a compelling vision.

It is now autumn in Scotland and as the nights grow long it is traditionally a time for storytelling. Scottish folk tales often feature aspects of the otherworldly: kelpies; selkies; witches and heroes with supernatural strengths.

It is this tradition and sense of myth that lies underneath Shoreline of Infinity – tales of wonder told around the fire as the cold wind swirls about us. The Beachcomber, who has lived on the shoreline of Infinity for time beyond time, sits at our fire of many colours, telling tales in a Universe of infinite possibilities.

Join us. Open this issue, and listen to your own inner voice as you read the wondrous tales from our latest gathering of brilliant storytellers: after all, the stories of unknown futures and alternative realities that constitute science fiction and fantasy are as much part of our tradition as any tales of beings shape-shifting from seal to human.

—Editor, September 2018

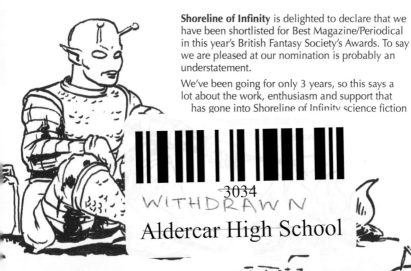

Shoreline of Infinity is delighted to declare that we have been shortlisted for Best Magazine/Periodical in this year's British Fantasy Society's Awards. To say we are pleased at our nomination is probably an understatement.

We've been going for only 3 years, so this says a lot about the work, enthusiasm and support that has gone into Shoreline of Infinity science fiction

Harry's Shiver

Esme Carpenter

Art: Jackie Duckworth Art

I 'm strapped up to my eyeballs in harnesses, clinging to the cliff-face below Castle Arco, trying very hard not to think about the small amounts of magnetic material in the rock that are currently gluing my electro-magnetised gloves to the wall.

Ancient Italy's Castle Arco is famously 'impossible to breach'. I love the word 'impossible' because, in its own finite and absolute way, it gives endless possibilities. Before space-travel and aliens and all of that craziness, our forefathers (in their wisdom) also used to say the *Titanic* was 'unsinkable', and that man on the moon was 'impossible', and that nobody would ever rob the Core-12 Space Station with only two pistols and a handful of Shivers.

I'm pleased to say that the Core-12 Space Station run was me.

I also love the word 'infamous'. That is what they call me nowadays. When I am the twitch of a shadow, I am the infamous Gure-Walker. When I am a whisper in an ear, I am the Thief Of Umbra. When I am a blip on a radar, I am Shiver. Nicknames are the best. I quite like Gure-Walker; it refers to my days living in the 'inhospitable' climate of the Gure Basin, where I quickly made a name for myself as a cutthroat. Thief Of Umbra is relatively ominous, but it's only because I stole the Umbra Maker of the Cult of Harrows and made a rather tidy profit on it.

Shiver is what I like the most. It takes my trademark tool and turns me into it. Shivers are largely overlooked by other thieves and spies, but I always make sure I have plenty with me. They can do so much that nobody has previously considered. Like I said, endless possibilities – given the right mindset and the quickest pair of hands.

Robbing the castle required preparation but I'm plenty used to that. Someone was willing to offer me a substantial amount of ticks for the job so it didn't take much persuasion. Tell me something's unbreachable and I'll breach it for you, if the money's right. I didn't get nicknames like Thief Of Umbra by shying away from difficult tasks. Unlike those hit-and-run guys, I take pride in my work. I plan, I practise, I theorise. I study history and war mechanics and all sorts. I had to talk to the right people and purchase or steal the correct equipment. I'm sure I've accounted for everything I could possibly account for, except failure.

I can't think about failure. Thinking about failure is like failure itself. The wind is sharp and taunting. How many feet up am I? No, don't think about that. Hand up. The only really comforting thought is that I can hear the electromagnets in the gloves whine when I put pressure against the rock. The harness contains the power packs and some of the climbing paraphernalia I've required up to this point. Right now, the only thing keeping me upright is the technology wrapped around my hands and the confidence that there's enough magnetic rock to keep me here.

The harness is chafing. I hope I can walk when I get up there.

My reasoning for being about two-hundred feet in the air relying on magnetic force is that Castle Arco has never successfully been stormed from the front before. Correct: *the front.* What army is ever going to think about scaling the cliff at the back? From here, it's a quick leap onto the battlements, a pause to shake the vertigo from your head, and away we go. The treasury is then on your immediate right, and with a little bit of perseverance you can definitely get in there and out in a fraction of the time.

I'm wondering why anyone would want to come here anymore anyway, despite the blindingly obvious. The hamlet that surrounds the castle is nigh on deserted (I can see it from the corner of my eye and am very sure I don't want to look down and investigate it any time soon). Only the castle is manned. The Porian Empire inhabited it after its capture of the planet; it's one of the strongholds that the Emperor's lackies squat in to ensure their safety. The hamlet was of little concern to them, and like most things of little concern to the Porian Empire, they trampled right through it and killed everyone in it. The rumour that the castle couldn't be attacked and would hold under siege comforted them greatly and because of this, unlike other castles and forts they've commandeered, they left Castle Arco much as it was when they found it, stoic and grand with its medieval features intact, save for preventative measures. The Porians dropped on it from above, and since then people tried space-drops with parachutes, but the anti-air lasers that were subsequently installed made bacon of them before they even hit the ground. That didn't stop anyone having a good go of it afterwards. Of course, direct assault was tried, and failed. Spies were always rooted out and publicly executed on holo-vision across the continent. As a result, most people leave the old relic alone. It looks like, to all intents and purposes, Castle Arco is the greatest stronghold of the entire Porian Empire.

This mixture of complacency and the promise of riches has kept people guessing for decades how to get inside. These sorts of complacencies make me tingle with excitement. They beg for my attentions. And when that gent came forward with all those ticks and told me all he wanted to get his hands on was a small orb, well, that was that.

Sweet stars, I *am* high up.

No, don't think about it. Look up. Above me I can see the trees. I'm almost there.

Finally, my hand makes contact with leaves – real leaves. I launch myself up and lie with my back against the rock, and sigh with relief. My arms and legs are shaking with exertion. It'll only take me a moment to recover myself.

Until then, I familiarise myself with my surroundings. Well, it certainly looks impressive from my perch at the top. Below me lies the castle, with its foreboding battlements and arrow slits, coupled with pieces of angular Porian technology designed to keep thieves like me out. I am well camouflaged in the trees, but there's no telling when the heat-seekers will find me out.

I content myself with stripping the gloves from my fingers and pulling all my harnesses off. I won't need them again. I drop them from the cliff and watch as they tumble into darkness. It's nice to feel light again, agile. I check my pockets for Shivers.

Shivers were invented to warn soldiers of enemy approach, like a sentient radar. They give off a little whine and shake alarmingly when certain heat signatures or pulse rates trigger them. If properly placed in a barracks, they could easily knock against pots and pans and alert the soldiers; they're tiny, and were rarely noticed by invaders. When the Porian Empire found out about them, they obviously became obsolete. Millions of the tiny blighters were lost to the back rooms of armourers and weapons technicians. Nobody saw the potential of the poor things.

Nobody but me.

A little tinkering, a few quick thoughts … a Shiver can do a hundred things it was never invented for.

I have twenty of them in my pockets. I've modified five types of Shiver for purposes known only to myself. The others are as the maker intended them to be. I attach one of the original Shivers to a tree beside me. It'll serve the double purpose of letting me know where to return to, and of confusing the heat-seekers and movement sensors of the guns on the battlements.

I begin.

My descent is short and sweet. I slip my Eye-Noc over my left eye. As I suspected, only four guards showing up in orange on my sensor. The Porians are relying heavily on the tech clinging like vultures to the medieval stone. I lift the Eye-Noc – its electrics can often alert sensors and I only use it when I have to – and make a slow way forward. My eyes adjust to the dark gradually and I can see them patrolling, hands loose on their weapons. I try to ignore the highest tower for now. Seeing my goal will only make me rush things. I need to focus on the task at hand.

I slide easily onto the battlements and crouch-run behind a gun. One of my precious Shivers needs to be sacrificed for a higher purpose (this always pains me; it's getting harder and harder to get my hands on working Shivers nowadays), and I think I can see the perfect way to do it.

Porian tech is something I marvel at, even years after their conquest. I'm used to their perfect angles and straight lines by now; the outside is always drab, sharp to remind you of their power. The inside, however … intricate glowing mazes of wires and knowledge. I ease the safety cover from the back of the gun and turn my Shiver on, and I slip it inside, shut the cover, and run to a shadowy corner.

Perfect timing, as usual. The trembles of the Shiver have caused something in the gun to come loose. It is failing, sparking, spinning around. The guard on this battlement is confused, and moves to check the gun.

So far, so good. I watch as the guard calls his comrades on his comms and their dutiful change of course towards the problem.

I make to run when the real fireworks begin. I wasn't expecting my little Shiver to do such amazing work. Whatever it knocked out wrecked the AI of the firing mechanism. The gun spins, and shoots a rogue blast. The guards are alarmed. I am increasingly impressed. The gun is going berserk, shooting, turning; the guards are hurrying about, trying to stop it or jump on it or shoot it. One of the shots hits another gun, which goes up in flames and sparks.

I can't help but smile. This is going far better than anticipated.

With the guards preoccupied, I can slip down the tower. This tower is hollow, save for steps; a lookout tower, with an arch at the bottom leading to the bridge across to the treasury. I jump steps and give up on whole flights altogether, landing cat-like on the next run. Before I hit the bottom, I toss a Shiver into the centre of the floor for good measure to attract the cameras, and hurry through the archway.

The Porians had the good sense to build a huge gate on the bridge. It's impressive, like most of their architecture, fashioned from Porian titanium and, judging by the muscular cables, full of electrics to keep it firmly shut. I would also wager it has weapons inside it if it's touched by human hand. A lot of Porian tech is wired to attack humans only; the slightest touch of human flesh on a piece of Porian metal could signal the end of your life.

Time for one of my modded Shivers. I call these ones Super Shivers. It takes only a quick reroute of power to make the trembling of the device useful for, say, messing up frequencies with intense, deep vibration. In the past I've used Super Shivers to cause blackouts, to jam communications. Today, I'm using one to shake up the lock mechanism of the gate.

I keep to the shadows. Cameras are advanced, but it'll take them some minutes to pick me up in the darkness, thanks to the shadow-sucking ultra-black of my outfit. I examine the gate. I can still hear the gun going off at the top of the tower and the guards crying out in panic. I have time. Eventually, I pick a spot where I can see a Porian finger is meant to fit perfectly. I attach the Super Shiver and retreat to the tower.

It takes a while. The Shiver whirs and works. Some of the lights in the gate begin to glow. The show is quite pretty as safeties go down and alarms are desensitised. The sound of creaking metal hits my ears. The gate shudders, and the jaws begin to open.

What's *that* sound?

I look up. One of the Porian guards is falling, rapidly, through the tower towards me.

I have few options available to me but to run. The gun must have shot him from the battlements. No doubt the rest of the guards will come to rescue his mangled corpse. It's safer by the gate.

I head into the shadows and manage to squeeze my body through the gate's gap. I daren't look back. Time to press on.

As I said, Castle Arco is vastly considered unbreachable. This wonderful ignorance means that I don't have to waste any more Shivers on the way to the treasury. The place is blissfully devoid of cameras and guns on the inside – and of soldiers, too. This is rapidly becoming one of the easiest jobs I've ever had to do. But no, I mustn't become a victim of that which I mock. I can't think that way. It would ruin me. I have to be on my guard.

Once, I believed I was home and dry. Once when I was younger. I failed to see the dangers of complacency for myself. I believed myself as untouchable as the white stone walls of Castle

Arco, back when I had no nicknames and no Shivers. Back when I was a petty thief.

Back when the Porians took my brother to shame me.

Never again.

I try not to imagine his face. I focus instead on entering the treasury. There is a door but I have a nagging hunch that this will be a flesh trigger. I attach a Shiver for good measure and see if the slight trembling will set anything off. Behind me, I can hear the guards' voices echo. By now they'll have realised the gate is open. I have to be quick.

The Shiver sets off a white-hot heat on the door. I raise my eyebrows – I've seen this once before – and I throw a Super Shiver to it, which opens it easily. I retrieve both Shivers (one is rendered useless from the heat, but the Super Shiver is salvageable) and go inside.

The treasury is cold and damp. I rig my Laser Shivers on either side of the door in case the guards follow me. Around me all I can see is a stone tower. I'm guessing there's some sort of hologram concealment in the room.

I relish the challenge. I place a couple of Shivers, see if the air moves when they tremble or if I dislodge pixels. Sure enough, there's a holo-ceal against the back wall. I gather up my babies and try to find the door-handle. The final Super Shiver works on the lock.

It's dark within. Too dark. I place my Eye-Noc on my eye and enter. It picks up the edges of stairs, going downwards; the cold is unbearable. A few times I lose my footing – the stairs are uneven – but I eventually find my way down. The sensor shows a final door and…

What? *Heat-signatures?*

I fiddle with the settings. No, the tech is picking up human heat. *Human* heat, not Porian heat.

My prize is waiting behind the door. I know it is. I pick it up and I leave here and the guy pays me my ticks and I retire rich and famous and far away from the Porian Empire and the ghost of my…

My brother.

The heat signatures remind me of my brother. They remind me of my continual nightmares about his daily torture. They remind me of the pain of not knowing what happened to him.

I fumble in my pocket. I know Harry's Shiver when I feel it in my hands. I lift it.

"Harry," I whisper to it, "find the people."

Harry's Shiver lifts from my palm, beeps a few blue lights, and shoots off to the left.

Harry's Shiver is a tracker. It is the first Shiver I ever saw. It is the one my brother gave me as a present, a token of something from long ago, when he didn't know I was stealing. When I lost him I modified it beyond recognition into something he would believe in. I follow it when I need to remember something higher than my glorified nicknames and my thrill-seeking, when conquering the unconquerable isn't enough. I may be the Gure-Walker and the Thief Of Umbra and Shiver, but I am also my brother's downfall. It is the one thing I must always remember. So I follow Harry's Shiver away from the door of the treasury and try to pick up pulse rates on my Eye-Noc so I can find out how many humans I'm dealing with.

I feel a prick on both of my wrists from my radar amulets. My heart drops. The Laser Shivers have been broken. The guards are coming.

And yet Harry's Shiver is still leading me, down this way and that, looking for people.

I don't have time for this. I don't know why I'm doing this. I came for a tiny ball, not for refugees. But my feet won't stop following. The glittering blue lights are leading me.

The heart rates finally pop up on my tech. Five. Five! Sweet stars, what am I doing? Harry's Shiver is waiting for me by the wall. The Eye-Noc can't see through walls, but it is showing pulse rates like there's no tomorrow. I take Harry's Shiver from the air.

"Good job, Harry."

The little blue lights shimmer happily.

I feel on the wall for a door-frame. I think the bricks come away in a block. I pull to my left; the wall gives. From the crack I can smell human sweat and excrement. I gag and keep pulling. In the low light beyond the wall I can see shapes. The Eye-Noc shows five thermal images of shaking, terrified human beings.

I put my finger to my lips. I think they see it because nobody speaks. I wave my hand, signalling that they stay down, and I back away into the tunnel.

I have to deal with the guards first. I rummage through my Shivers for my Bomb Shivers and sigh at the thought of wasting them. The image of my brother comes to me again, and I click the timer for two minutes.

I place the Bomb Shivers on the door to the treasury and back away. The Eye-Noc will show me clearly when the Porians are close. The two minutes might be too short. I crouch, feeling the burn in my legs from the climb and the dread in my heart at how I'm losing out on all those ticks, when the Porian guards come clattering down the stairs, right to the treasury.

The explosion blinds me and the Eye-Noc for a brief moment. My ears ring. When I shake the stars from my eyes I can see the explosion has done the trick. I back down the tunnel for my charges and usher them from their prison. They're weak, can barely move; I have to practically carry two down the corridor. I tell them how to escape and where they can find help, but they look at me with wet eyes and I know I can't leave them on their own. I glance through the blown-up door. I can see the small orb in a glass case at the end of the room.

I climb the stairs. It hurts to leave all those ticks behind. I aid my stragglers up into the top room and chaperone them through the gate, collecting all my Shivers on the way. I pause at the gate, look back. I could still grab it and get all of us out.

I *have* to grab it.

But I can't. Alarms will be ringing and guards will undoubtedly come now there's been an explosion. The job is done.

I take the refugees up the stairs to the top of the tower, shield them from the crazy gun, and take them up the hill to where my final Shiver rests, trembling at our return.

I take it from the tree. My stomach feels heavy. I think of my brother. He would probably assume I did the right thing.

My transport is descending. The driver I paid looks shocked when he sees me with all these dirty humans but he takes us all in regardless. I sit at the open door and stare out at Castle Arco.

There is weight on my hand. I turn. One of the humans – a girl – is sitting beside me. She has her hand on mine and her emaciated face sports a grateful smile. She looks beautiful for a moment.

"Thank you," she says.

I think of Harry and I nod.

"You're safe now," I say.

"What do we call our saviour?" she asks.

I almost laugh when she calls me that. It's as if she thinks I went there to rescue them, to liberate them from the unbreachable castle and come back a hero. But I suppose that's what I've done.

I would want someone to do the same for Harry.

"My name is Amber. But please ... call me Shiver."

Esme Carpenter started writing science-fiction and fantasy aged 12 and found she couldn't stop. This momentum took her to the University of East Anglia to study Creative Writing, and onwards to teach English. While originally from York, England, she moved to California, USA eighteen months ago to be with her husband.

The Time Between Time

Premee Mohamed

Art: Becca McCall

Sponsored by Martyn Turner

Dalton was looking for interesting bugs on the tree when the window appeared beneath her fingertips. She jerked her hand back so fast that she nearly hit herself in the face, then blinked repeatedly to make sure she wasn't imagining it. But no, there it was: the size of a postage stamp, transparent, the cool surface glass-smooth.

"Holy sh –" she whispered, then cut herself off as if her parents were listening, though they had left for work hours ago. She felt lightheaded, realized she was holding her breath, forced herself to breathe.

She went up on tiptoe, slowly, though no-one had ever heard of the windows vanishing once they had appeared, and put one eye to it.

This would be a good one, she could tell. An endless plain of purple grass, flecked with crimson and palest pink, studded with half-hidden petals. The sky was the now-familiar turquoise, lit with a tiny or distant sun. Water shimmered in the near distance – or was it? There was a heaviness to its movements, as if it were not water at all but something denser, richer – blood, oil, mercury. Dalton's skin prickled as something moved through the tall grass. There – a head poking through the vegetation, all hexagons and horns, like a bee crossed with an elk. The –

"Dalton! You all right, honey?"

"Yes, Mrs Li!" she called back, jerking away from the tree, heart hammering. "Just found a cool bug!"

"Don't bring it in the house!"

Dalton waved politely, then returned to her book until Mrs Li went back inside. Technically, Dalton was a latchkey kid for the summer, but non-technically she wasn't *home alone* as long as their neighbour kept half an eye on her when she was in the backyard. Which was going to be most of the time; there was nothing to do inside. It was better to take her bug-catcher and magnifying glass and ID books and load her phone with bird-call mp3s and spend hours mildly harassing the natural world. Had she found an interesting bug, it would certainly have gone into the house, at least for the afternoon; instead, she'd found something much better, something almost no one had.

The first one had supposedly appeared about three months ago, but really it was just the first reported to the media. It was always possible that some had appeared earlier, in places unseen or unreported. Dalton always reminded people of that; a fanatical reader of 'National Geographic,' she knew there were places that people couldn't or wouldn't go, still, in this age of double-digit billions of people. But as soon as that first one was publicised, it had set off a worldwide search for the things – jungle cruises, desert expeditions, drone flybys. Her parents, a physicist and biologist, had been pulled into newsrooms and podcasts to talk about them. But what was there to say? Everything was conjecture. That, Dalton explained smugly to her friends, meant *guess*.

Her class had begged for a day off school to look around Edmonton for one of the windows – you never knew where they'd turn up! – and been denied, and there had almost been a mutiny, but classes were almost over by then. And anyway, people had started setting up tiny cameras, pinpoint-small, to create livestreams of the more interesting ones. But nothing, she'd heard over and over, *nothing* beat looking into one for real, and she understood that now.

She crept back to the window, her fingers exploring the seamless edges against the bark. More animals had arrived on the other side – shuffling giant millipedes, corpulent and glossy; the bee-elk, dipping their elegant, large-eyed heads to the water; something clearly predatory, low and clawed, in an uneasy peace with the others, its fangs so long they sank into the scarlet mud.

The watering-holes were the best windows, everyone agreed; just like here, they attracted animals for miles around.

They weren't here, though. The early ones, often showing dunes or stones, could have been from anywhere on Earth; experts immediately began to use satellite images and AI algorithms trying to find matching landmarks. It almost became a game, quietly frantic behind the scenes. Dalton had watched her dad and his friends in the kitchen, pulling data and watching live feeds of a dozen windows, trying to calculate day length, star positions, shadow angles. Maybe one day they would know exactly where it was; in the meantime, the xenobiological and astronomical communities had settled on 'Not-Earth,' and someone on Twitter had started calling it 'Planet X'.

Dalton watched the window all day, going inside only to make lunch and bring it outside, along with her sketchbook and pencil crayons so she could try to draw the creatures pacing to and from the water hole like clockwork. Some of the really good windows, like hers, had become swamped with visitors in the early days, succumbing to the hysteria of it all, the excitement, the hope; people had tried to fence them off or charge admission.

A few folks had gotten sick of the attention their windows attracted, and tried to paint over them. But anything that touched the glass-like material – even fingerprints, Dalton now noticed, or noseprints – simply erased itself after a few minutes. Blink, and gone. In the space between seconds, Stephen Hawking had said; and no one knew what that meant, only that Dalton's dad had spent about three weeks revising next year's curriculum, because everything had changed. It seemed obvious that it was happening in time – one second there, the next not. Yet even if you filmed it, you couldn't pin down exactly when it happened.

Tick, tick, tick. That's where the windows ran – on their own time, in the commas between the ticks.

She thought she'd never tire of just staring into the wonder of the window, gaping at the things it showed, but a week later, she texted her best friend Tate: *Can you keep a secret?*

He wrote back: *Coming over!!*

She dragged a brush through her dark hair and swapped her syrup-stained t-shirt for a clean one, thinking, *Don't make me regret this.* Tate wasn't necessarily her *best* best friend; that was Jenny, who had moved away two years ago and whose absence she still keenly felt. But he had the advantages of proximity and malleability, and he genuinely liked, or at least was capable of acting as if he liked, Dalton's effusive nerdery on topics ranging from string theory to convergent evolution, interpreted through an eleven year-old's precocious but imprecise vocabulary. She had lots of friends at school, but summers were different somehow. People you hung out with every day disappeared for two months, reappearing in September transformed and casual, and identifiably someone else.

Tate was suitably awed by the window – perhaps overawed, as he stumbled back from his first starving stare into it, ten minutes long, and tripped over a root. "I can't *believe* you got one!"

"I know! People keep saying they're showing up randomly."

"I guess aliens don't know if they're going somewhere where people would see them or not," Tate said, glancing back at it. "Did you tell your mom and dad?"

"Of course not."

"But this is what your dad *does!*" Tate protested, then chewed his lip thoughtfully. "At least, I think. He tried to tell me that one time at dinner."

"Yeah, I didn't understand any of that either," Dalton admitted. "But I found it, so it's mine."

"It's their *tree.*"

"It's not their tree. They didn't pay for it."

"They're paying for the house."

"It's not about money," Dalton said firmly. "It's about *finder's rights.* I read about it."

Tate gave up, and turned his gaze back to the window, which reflected for a moment his gold-green eye and freckled cheek. He scratched at the clear surface with his fingernail. "There's people in Europe trying to send stuff through them, I read," he said.

21

"I read about that too. Switzerland. They built some kind of … miniature particle accelerator in a field or something."

"But they said they don't know if it's working."

"My dad says transporting any kind of particle doesn't count until you can send a grapefruit through."

"Why a grapefruit?" said Tate.

"I have no idea." Dalton pushed him gently aside and took a turn – nothing now but a couple of the millipedes, brick-red with sky-blue eyes. "The whole world changed, Tate. There's cults now, about these things. I seen 'em on Dr. Phil. Religion changed, physics changed. Proof we're not alone."

"*Aliens,*" he said, drawing the word out slowly. "Except, I heard someone saying yesterday that they're not really windows into an alien planet. That it's still Earth, but in an alternate timeline."

"Of course it's not Earth," Dalton said. "People keep trying to prove it, and they can't."

"Not our Earth. Another Earth. A different one." He turned back to her. "I can't believe you've had it this long and didn't tell me!"

"Well, I didn't tell anyone else, either," she said. He beamed, his blush radiating up into his glasses and filling them with pink. "It's pretty cool though. We could charge like, hundreds of dollars for people to come look in this one."

"Yeah! Half of the ones I watch don't have anything in them. There's a desert one where you can sometimes see these big ants."

"Ants are cool," Dalton said briskly. "Remember last year, when we –"

"Mom said I'm not allowed to talk about that any more."

Tate came over every day after that, and they spent a week extensively analyzing and documenting everything they saw, taking turns as their eyes tired. Dalton's mom, as she fed them dinner in the big, bay-windowed kitchen, often commented on how strung-out they looked. "We're getting *outdoor activity* as per the *Health Canada guidelines for children*, Mom," Dalton announced. Mom rolled her eyes, but gave them second helpings and let them take Melona bars for dessert.

Afterwards they raced back outside to station themselves under the tree, swinging aside the chip of bark Dalton insisted they pin up to keep it covered. They hid from the infrequent spatters of July-warm rain beneath the thick foliage, backs to the trunk, feeling the rough heat of the day through their t-shirts, and talked quietly about going to the big-kid junior high next year, and possible outfit schemes, clique management, and survival strategies.

"We should build a treehouse," Tate said. "So we don't have to go back inside so much. We could sleep –"

"Dad wouldn't let me," Dalton said. "I already asked."

"My parents wouldn't notice," Tate said.

"Well we didn't find a window at your house, did we?"

They used Tate's phone to follow the breathless progress of windows research; his phone was old, but it didn't have all the locks, blocks, and tracers that Dalton's did. She couldn't have explained why she was so invested in not having her parents know about the window, but she dug her heels in against the idea, and felt sick every time she thought about telling. Anyway, the aliens had given *her* the window, hadn't they?

Some people, she and Tate read, didn't believe it was aliens at all – there was the alternate-Earth timeline, and there were those who insisted they were glimpses of heaven, in preparation for the imminent Second Coming, or Hell, ditto, or Valhalla. Or a high-tech prank (Dalton was a strong proponent of this one, though it saddened her to think Planet X wasn't real) or hoax, or a marketing stunt, or the work of hyperintelligent Earth bees or ants. "Not wasps, obviously," Tate said. "Wasps are stupid."

"Wasps aren't any stupider than bees."

"Well, they don't know how to make honey."

"Neither do you."

You couldn't destroy the windows, they read, and to their astonishment several people had been hurt firing guns at them and having the bullets ricochet; nothing showing intelligence had yet been seen through a window; one had been found set up very high on the other side, so that you could see over a long, curved horizon. Something that tantalizingly resembled a city smoked far in the distance. And why were they so *small*? Were the aliens small? Could they see Earth from their side – a gamut of lineups, gawking eyes, and ordinary life?

"We could ask someone to set up a pincam at this one," Tate said once, and Dalton quietly told him to shut up. He didn't ask again, though he did ask to visit her dad's office with her one day when they both had headaches from staring into the tiny glass pane. She indulged him, though her mom's lab was much more interesting: tobacco plants and canola and tomato and Arabidopsis, smelling of chemicals and the incongruous sweetness of green growing things all year round. Dad's was just full of books. They played with the whiteboard while he taught his summer-semester class, drawing animals no-one would recognize and talking about science as if they knew what any of the words in the books meant. But it couldn't last.

One Saturday, Dalton woke up to voices in the backyard, and tiptoed to her parted blinds, telling herself it wasn't what it sounded like, it was a coincidence, Mrs Li had visitors, anything but *that*. Instead: two heads craning to look at the window in the tree, its bark covering tossed aside. She even recognized them – Sierra, a girl from Tate's street who he'd been in love with for years, identifiable from her long, dark, shining hair, and Jay, who lived closer to the student residences. Dalton stared, her mouth filling with sour spit, chest hitching. Tate must have told, the little traitor. After all they'd seen, after all they'd shared! How could he?

She thought of some stupid video they'd watched, about the hope for Planet X, about how it united the entire human race in looking towards the future. Well, that was *crap*. The entire human race didn't *deserve* Planet X. And certainly not these two, walking into her backyard like they owned the place!

Damage control, that was the phrase she was trying to remember. The damage had been done, but maybe there was still time to control it.

Dressed, teeth brushed, still trembling, she strolled outside with a broad smile on her face, and savoured Sierra's guilty jump as the back door clicked shut. "Hey guys!"

"Hi!" Sierra said, and there was a pause as they sized each other up, tried to figure out who was in the wrong, who had the power, just like on the playground every day. The damp grass came up to their ankles, each shadow yards long in the morning light. Dalton's dad had been too busy to mow lately.

Eventually, Dalton managed to convince them that they were in a club now – the Secret Window Club – and that they must each speak a fearsome oath to secrecy, using the well-known pinky swear. "If you break it, I get to break your pinky," Dalton said.

"I know *that*," Sierra said, annoyed.

"I know a kid who did it," said Jay, holding his hand out next, sticky with sap.

"I've done it," Dalton lied coolly. "It doesn't take much. It's like breaking a popsicle stick. Pinky bones are pretty small." She'd like to break Tate's pinky, she thought, but she hadn't made him swear anything. She'd *trusted* him. Well, that was a mistake she wouldn't make again. Just as long as these two didn't talk.

But the damage had clearly been done; by Sunday afternoon, the backyard was packed with sightseers, researchers, reporters, neighbourhood kids. They came in a trickle at first, speaking in low voices, and then around dinnertime it was as if a dam had burst. Her parents walked back from the train station just in time for the news van to pull up, nudging through the queue.

Dalton tried to explain as they came in, managing only to point and blurt, "Planet X!"

Dad bolted for the backyard, admitting a golden swell of light that filled the kitchen like water. Mom stayed at the counter, and put the kettle on.

"Is he getting rid of them?" Dalton asked, not turning around. She felt perilously close to tears.

Her mom gave her a look. "What's up, chicken butt?"

"Nothing."

"Uh huh. You want a cup of tea?"

"It's not theirs!" Dalton burst out. "Why can't we just tell them to leave?"

"Well, we could do that," her mom said placidly. "Or we could do like everybody else is doing, and let people look."

"We don't have to! *You* always told me to follow my heart, no matter what other people were doing!"

"Yes, we did," her mom said, and looked up at the ceiling. "But uh, I'm starting to think maybe we worded that wrong."

"Movies say the same thing, Mom. Why would they tell kids that if it wasn't true?"

"You remember where I used to live, baby? Out by the train station? Well, every couple weeks I'd come home and there'd be a sheriff's van there pulling in or pulling out. With people being let out of the remand centre, the one out by Fort Sask."

"So?"

"So listen," her mom said, plopping teabags into mugs. "The sheriffs would lead them out of the van and give them a gift card or some cash – twenty bucks, it looked like. And then they'd drive off again. That's all some people got, when they got back to the world. Twenty bucks and a handshake."

"So? So *what*? Our yard isn't –"

"Some people have things other people don't have, OK?" her mom sighed. "I'm saying that if you've got those things, even if you got them given to you, maybe *especially* if they were given to you, you owe it to the world to give to people who don't. Otherwise, what kind of world is it? How can it all work?"

Dalton stared at her, wounded. Finally she murmured something about her sketchbook, and plodded upstairs, where she watched the crowd eddy and swirl around her tree in the backyard, like ants converging around a dropped bit of food. There were drones in the air now, their tiny lenses throwing back the late-afternoon light like gold coins. She debated throwing something at them, then decided against it. She might get in trouble.

What did her mom know, anyway? All this *given to you* business. Unlike Dalton's dad, her mom's parents had emigrated to Canada with nothing – one suitcase between the two of them, fleeing a country where they'd eaten garbage and songbirds to survive. Surely after a lifetime of hearing those stories, Dalton's mom would understand that if you did have something like this – something priceless, amazing – the last thing you should do was hand it off like an unwanted present. If you kept doing that, you'd have nothing!

Tate returned the next afternoon, edging through the crowd with his hands up to show he wasn't butting in line, and into the house. One of Dalton's dad's friends waved as he went past; she'd offered to install a pincam on their window to see if it would reduce the crowds a little. It was either that, they agreed, or try to hire some private security – at least for the family that lived in their basement suite, if not for themselves. They were old, the lodgers, and slept lightly; Dalton had sneaked downstairs once to look for a book in the storage room, and woken Mr Petryk with the sound of her socked feet on the carpet.

Dalton rounded on Tate now, seeing that he was trailed by Sierra and Jay – who he had, she was sure, brought as shields, expecting a deflection of her righteous rage. It wouldn't help.

"I can't believe you told!"

"I never said I wasn't going to!"

"Well *I* never said it was OK!"

"Why would *you* have to tell me that?" Tate shouted, surprising her. She'd expected at least the pretense of remorse.

Were the drones outside recording? She didn't care. Let the whole world hear how right she was! Maybe someone would hear it, and tomorrow there would be an article about it.

"Why *wouldn't* I?!"

"We're not supposed to be told!" Tate cried. "We're supposed to just *know to share stuff* by now! And you never do! People still have to tell you to! And then you hate it!"

"No I don't!"

From the corner of her eye, Dalton became aware that Sierra and Jay were backing off, hands slightly up, as if from an angry dog. That made her even madder: who was going to attack *them*? They weren't even part of this!

"You do too!" Tate snarled. "And you've never had to share anything in your whole life, and that's why you're mad!"

"Oh, you liar! You liar. I have to share everything!"

"Name one thing!"

"Well I have to share my mom and dad with the stupid university!" she yelled. "I have to share my house with the Petryks! I had to share my window! And thanks to you, I have to share my backyard with all these strangers!"

"None of that's yours! You've never had to share anything that was yours! You've never had to give up anything, not one single thing, so that someone else could have it. That's your problem, Dalton Harris," he finished triumphantly, though tears now sheeted down his face like cellophane. "You're *selfish*."

Her mouth snapped shut as if she'd been slapped, cutting off her reply midway through not even a word but a syllable. Sierra made a dismissive gesture, her face smug, and left, dragging the still-interested Jay.

Dalton inhaled to defend herself, then exhaled. The backyard noises receded into her ringing ears. She thought about Tate's parents, who also worked at the university, behind desks rather than microscopes, and how she'd known that before but never thought about it; about his brothers and sister, their bunkbed-crammed rooms, the backyard churned into mud from the constant pressure of running feet.

"Look, just because," she began, and trailed off. Tate stomped into his shoes, crushing both back heels, and shuffled stiffly off the back porch, not looking back. In a moment he was lost in the crowd.

The window vanished as suddenly as it had appeared, which Dalton only realized when she woke up to silence, rather than the restrained hum of the usual early-morning watchers. Not quite: she drew her blinds and saw one man, youngish, maybe a student, bumbling around on the lawn. He looked up when he saw Dalton peering through the screen.

"Isn't this the watering hole window?" he yelled.

"Yeah," she called back.

He mumbled something and resumed his search, crawling his hands along the trunk in a way that she did not at all like, the long pale fingers too spiderlike against the darkness. But it was really gone. She could tell from a single glimpse, the absence of those small hard lines against the flowing grain of the bark.

Downstairs, she made oatmeal and sat in the living room. It must have happened before her parents left for work; the thick blackout blinds had been taken down, folded in the corner next to the couch. The lace curtains remained, billowing in the warm breeze. Dalton turned on the TV for the noise.

There. All over the world, the little windows had vanished. Gone in an instant, or between two instants, just like everything else they did. The hundreds of streams showed only Earth now: exaggerated closeups of brick, tile, metal, glass, bark, asphalt, stone. She allowed herself a single wild flare of hope as something moved across one of the feeds, but it was just an iridescent green beetle, hugely magnified into an alien. She closed her eyes and imagined the thick lilac grass again, the familiar shape of the pool, the moving mouths of the animals sending ripples towards her.

"Will we ever get another glimpse of Planet X?" the pretty newscaster said, and Dalton shook her head, and only then realized she was crying into her breakfast. She swiped angrily at her cheeks. She'd been crying a lot these last two weeks, quietly, in the blanket fort she'd built in her room. Her eyes hurt now, and she hadn't hidden it as well as she'd hoped; her parents had tried to get her to see their family doctor, but she'd managed to keep putting it off.

Will we ever? meant *never*.

They were lost forever, more than lost, it was as if they had never existed at all – never mind the recordings, the articles, the books that had already come out. And yet, at least they were all gone together, no exceptions. And there was plenty of data to work with. Maybe people would figure out where Planet X was later, given all that. Maybe the world could rally around that instead. Dalton told herself all this, trying to be logical, scientific, the way Mom and Dad would tell her to be, but it didn't help. She sobbed and finished her oatmeal and returned to the kitchen for something else to eat, even though she was full.

Her phone pinged; she took it off the charger pad and read the message through her tears.

Heard about the windows?!

Tate. It had been so long since his last text that for the first time in her memory, there was a block of empty space between the messages. As if he too had been yanked from the sky by mischievous aliens, and suddenly returned. Unasked-for, unprompted.

Yes, she wrote back. *Sucks.*

A pause. She held her breath, thumbs poised. There was so much more she wanted to say, though she acknowledged it would fall short of the cacophony in her head – despair, grief, numbness, yearning. She wanted to write *I missed you.* And *I'm sorry* and *I think I get it* and *Is it OK now? Are we OK? Will we hurt each other any more?*

Instead she waited, and watched the screen, and heard the man outside leave, clicking the back gate shut.

Premee Mohamed is an Indo-Caribbean scientist and spec fic writer based in Canada. Her work has been published by *Automata Review, Mythic Delirium, Pseudopod, Nightmare Magazine,* and others.
She can be found on Twitter at @premeesaurus.

Can Science Fiction Save Us?
Shoreline of Infinity Edinburgh International Science Festival Special Issue

paperback, 190pages £10
Available in all bookshops and from our website
Also available in PDF, ePub and Kindle versions

www.shorelineofinfinity.com

Stories and poems by

Jane Alexander

Charlie Jane Anders

Eric Brown

Anne Charnock

David L Clements

Leigh Harlen

Ian Hunter

Ken MacLeod

Tim Major

Paul McAuley

Colin McGuire

Megan Neumann

Jennifer R. Povey

Juliana Rew

Peter Roberts

Michael F Russell

Holly Schofield

Marge Simon

Guy Stewart

Adrian Tchaikovsky

JS Watts

Davyne DeSye

Jane Yolen

Victoria Zelvin

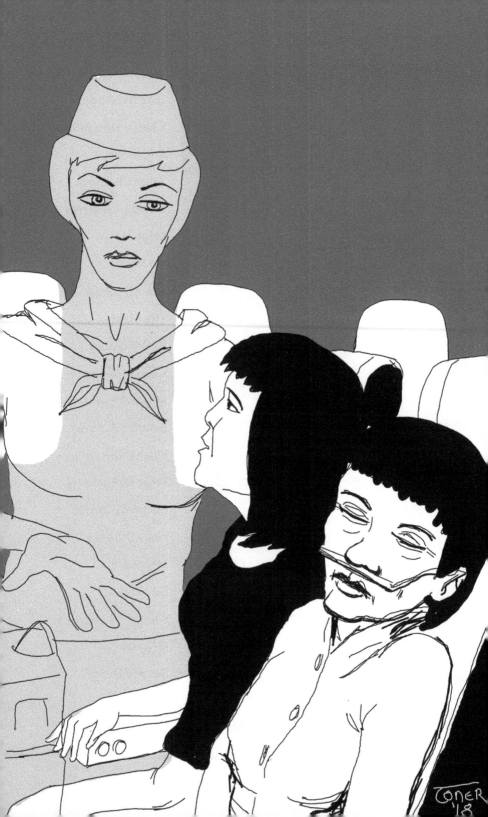

Daughter

Laura Young

Art: Mark Toner

娘

Seven years, **Umi's mother had said** to her daughter, her voice balancing in the fragile space she held for her only child. *Seven years you have been gone. Umi-chan, I don't know how much time I have left. But please, Umi, leave me here to die.*

Umi flipped through SkyMall. If she had that fountain, the table-top one, she could put it on the corner of her desk next to the aralia, still in its original pot. She bought it on her third day in San Francisco, down at the Ferry Building which her new neighbor Lindsay had told her about. Already homesick—or heartsick—he had taken the 38 Geary early that morning, hoping to find some hon dashi like her grandmother would make. This was before she knew the best dashi was only two streets over from her new apartment. She hadn't believed her mother when she'd assured Umi she'd feel at home after some time. *It will take some time. Think of* Otō-san, her mother had said and contacted everyone her father had ever known in America—even those from the prison camps—trying to do what she could from so far away with so little. Umi knew the money was too good to pass up. What she would be able to send home rectified any lingering hesitation about taking the position to code at NeoCore; she had even been excited about the biometric possibilities she'd have access to. That high had lasted only as long as the plane and car ride, though, before her sadness, the inescapable suffering she had felt as long as she could remember, pressed down upon her, making her feel as though she had risen too fast from the earth.

Her mother stirred next to her. Her breathing was loud and labored and even in her sleep she sounded like she was suffocating. Umi should've offered her something, one of her Xanaxes or Clonazapems, but she didn't want her to know she'd been to a Western doctor or that he had waved a small slip of paper toward her and told her that her attention should improve within a few weeks, though the depression would take a little longer. But that was three months ago and still her synapses flicked and burst, still the floating greyness fell around her. He'd told her to come back when she was feeling better, that then they could get at the root of her other problems, which she had purposefully left off the questionnaire. How could she put into writing *my father* and *now my mother* and *what will be left when everything is gone?*

"Something to drink?"

Umi looked up at the woman. Dressed in a classic navy ensemble, her floral scarf was immaculately tied around her neck, the ends of which barely graced her shoulder. The hues suited her.

"Jin, onegaishimasu,"

"Hai," the attendant replied.

How easily the words had come out. For the duration of the flight she would need to speak in her mother tongue, her father's antiquated Tohoku-ben. And here was a woman, a beautiful woman, with her British-born accent, smiling, always smiling, as she scooped three or four ice cubes and shook them into a plastic cup, handing it and a small bottle of Tanqueray to Umi.

She leaned over and rummaged in her purse with her free hand, hearing the pills bounce around in their plastic bottles. Careful not to knock her mother's elbow or knee and without taking her hands out of the bag, she opened the small bottle and shook out one, two, three small white pills into her sweaty palm. She coughed into her fist just long enough to get them into her mouth. Then she took a sip, a large one, from her cup before pulling down the tray on the back of the seat. She put her drink in the round divot, pushing it around to make sure it was stable and leaned her head back, waiting waiting waiting for the grey to fall around her, the only embrace she could remember.

She woke with a start, feeling the plane shudder deep inside a dreamless sleep. It made her heart leap and her stomach fall as they lost altitude so quickly. Umi checked the other passengers for any signs of alarm, but she saw only a cabin full of sleeping men and women, their heads tossed back, their mouths open, illuminated by the glow of the seatbelt indicators and frozen video screens. They looked like statues, eternally discomforted and still. The plane hummed and the white noise of the ventilation drowned out the breathing and wheezing and snoring of the others. Umi checked the valve on her mother's oxygen tank. There was enough, even if they were diverted or stalled in a landing pattern. She turned on her own video screen and saw not the flight path or advertisements, but a long scroll of code.

As she started to read it, she brought her purse up to her lap and opened her pill case. One Adderall, one Abilify, one Zoloft. Her survival cocktail. She took them at once, downing the dry pills with her watered down, lukewarm gin. She had missed dinner service and was starving. Soon the beautiful woman would come down the aisle, pushing a cart and offering a continental breakfast or the seafood and rice. She could smell it warming up, floating through the air ducts back toward her seat. It smelled like her mother's cooking, cooking Umi was never able to replicate in San Francisco, no matter how she tried. Maybe it had been the village well water, or the chives that grew outside her door, or the eggs fresh from the pen behind her home. But Umi's attempts tasted too clean, too refined, and lacked the earthy, animalistic freshness of something five minutes dead. Her mother slaughtered fast, landing the meat in the pan within minutes of taking its life.

Umi's eyes quickly skimmed over the code. Looked like a connection break and reload. But there at the end was an error message: flight completed. Then she saw the date at the bottom of the screen. It was June 28—her father's birthday—but the screen said it was 2037. She read it again, worried that something had happened to the computer system and then reached over to turn on her mother's screen. It had the same message. That couldn't be right. She checked her watch. One hour left.

"Okā-chan," Umi said, softly rubbing her mother's arm. "Wake up. We'll be landing soon."

Her mother opened her eyes, taking a moment to focus them on her daughter. Her oxygen tube had slipped from her nose in her sleep and Umi helped put it back into place. As she did so, her mother's chest swelled and she quickly brought her hand to her mouth, trying in vain to cover the coughing fit that took over. Umi reached into the pocket of her mother's suit jacket and took out the lace handkerchief, the one with the details she remembered from her childhood and held it up to her mother's face. Her mother took it and nearly shoved it in her mouth, coughing and coughing, a scourge inside of her, the same one that took her father.

"Umi," her mother said in between coughs, "Water, please."

She reached up and pressed the call button, waiting anxiously for the beautiful woman to reappear before her. As she waited she thought of Brianna, of her long hair and the way she'd stretch in the morning when she woke. It'd been three months and not one text message. That was what Umi wanted—staying friends would be too difficult. But now, knowing her mother would be staying with her indefinitely, she was thankful she wouldn't need to explain Brianna's presence in her cramped apartment. It was just as well that neither ever knew about the other.

She pressed the call button again and then remembered that she had a small bottle of water in her purse. She took it out and handed it to her mother, then watched her sip the water, taking it in between her thin lips, the skin around them creased and dry. Her mother had been forty-four when she'd had Umi, years after she'd had the last of seven miscarriages. The doctor had told her she was broken—*owatta*, her mother had said. But either she wasn't or Umi healed her; her mother believed her daughter was a harbinger of good fortune and for several years after she was born, the family was happy. But Otō-san got sick, and then he couldn't work. They had to sell the land—the land of her father's father, but it didn't matter because even if they could've afforded the treatment it would have been of little use, his lungs already a lace of tissue.

Umi rang the call button again—where was the flight attendant? She looked back over her seat, but saw no movement in the back, so she crawled over her mother and walked up to the front of the plane and there, where the flight attendants should have been, was an empty galley. There were cups of water on the steel counter and she took two.

"Would you care for a snack?"

Umi turned around, but saw no one there. Suddenly the panel above the counter lit up, displaying images of bags of chips and candy bars and fresh fruit, and again she heard "Would you care for a snack?" She realized the voice was coming from a speaker on the display, a vending machine of sorts. She looked up at it and then tapped on the cashews. A smiley emoji appeared and a drawer popped open in front of her, revealing small bags of nuts. She took one and the drawer closed. Where was the breakfast service? They should've been going up and down the aisles by now.

Back at her seat, she handed the cashews to her mother. What was she going to do now that her mother was going to live with her? She hadn't had to watch her father die—she was away at university. She could only imagine what her mother's gasping breath would sound like in her small apartment. Umi would take the couch until—if—her mother was moved to a hospice.

"We are beginning our descent into San Francisco." It was a recording, not the same voice as the flight attendant. Umi reached for the tray table, but it began to move, folding up into a small square before inserting itself into a small space in the back of the chair in front of her. Either she hadn't noticed it before, or she was losing her mind because she remembered pulling the tray down from the back of the seat. She was starving, probably hallucinating. She felt her seat straighten to its upright position, but she hadn't pressed the button. She looked at her mother, so frail and ashen, but her eyes were closed again.

The first thing she noticed was the terminal. It had changed since last week—drastically—and though thousands of people walked quickly to and from their flights, Umi couldn't find anyone in a uniform; there was no one to ask about her baggage. There were no counters at the gates, no shopkeepers hawking their goods. Instead there were kiosks. Gleaming, chest high compartments spanning the length of the terminal. And as Umi looked down the corridor and back, she lost count of how many there were. On the wall beyond the kiosks she saw nothing but green. It took her a minute to realize it was an expansive living wall. She could smell water. And mud. And for a moment she was back in Senboku, with her father in the garden. She could see his hunched back and the wad of fabric in his hand that he brought to his mouth every so often, making sure to put it away quickly so that Umi would not see the blood.

"Okā-chan, did you hear where our baggage would be?"

"No, I had my aids turned down."

Umi went up to one of the kiosks and put her finger on the spot of the screen that said "touch here". The kiosk rose up, extending on a cylinder until it was at eye level.

"Please look forward," it said. Must be a new security system. After all, it had been a long time since Umi had been to the international terminal. She had flown domestic and connected in New York on the way there.

She did as directed, and there was a flash. Jolted, she stepped back, nearly onto her mother's toes. "Haha, do you see this?" But her mother was busy putting on her disposable face mask.

"You don't need that here," Umi said. Her mother ignored her and strung it around her ears.

"Please remain at this kiosk," the voice from the computer said. "Your baggage is scheduled to arrive in two minutes."

"What?" Umi muttered and then, out of the corner of her eye, she saw what reminded her of a tiny flatbed truck, a miniaturized version. On the bed were two suitcases. It stopped at the kiosk next to her and her mother, and a couple—perhaps newly married or still simply smitten with one another—took the bags off the contraption and went on their way.

"No way," Umi said. "Did you see that? They bring the baggage to you," and as the words fell from her mouth their own bags arrived, Umi's dirty and scuffed and her mother's just purchased. She looked at the signs hanging above her head, even though she knew how to get to the subway.

"Come on, we're taking BART back to my place."

"Bart?"

"The train."

Umi knew her mother wasn't comfortable in small spaces or tunnels or anything in which she could not easily see a way out, so she hadn't told her before. But it was the only option since Umi did not own a car and taking a taxi—or even an Uber or Lyft—was fairly expensive. Though now, seeing her mother's condition, she had second thoughts. She took her phone out to order a car service, but it was dead.

"It'll be fine," Umi said to her mother. "It's fast and it's not usually crowded."

Her mother remained silent but allowed Umi to take her by the arm. They took an escalator down underneath the runways and terminals to the station where they waited for the train. They walked slowly, her mother stopping every few yards to catch her breath. Each time, Umi's stomach folded and knotted deep inside of her. She was losing her mother.

They boarded with bags in hand and the doors closed behind them. The seats were cushioned, lined up against the sides of the trains, leaving the passengers to look one another in the eyes. Above their heads were advertisements. Television screens flashed with products available, city monuments to visit, and restaurants to dine at. The city must've remodelled the subway system since it was much nicer than she'd remembered. She double checked that they were on the right one—red Richmond Line—and she thought of the photos she'd sent her mother over the years. Would she think that Kinokuniya Mall was too Americanized? Would she be able to hear Umi's ancestral tongue slipping in favor of the West? Or would she not concern herself with such things, thinking only how long it would be before she met Otō-san once again, somewhere above the mountaintops of Kyoto?

Her mother coughed and held on to Umi's forearm. Then, from a few seats over, a small white plastic block on wheels rolled out and came towards their feet. Umi's heart leapt thinking only of the terror cells that had been foiled in surrounding neighborhoods, of what she heard on the news, of unattended packages and suspicious behavior, but as far as she could tell, no one paid attention to the rolling cube that stopped at the feet of her mother. A small compartment opened and on a panel was a flashing picture of a hand.

"Please insert palm," it directed and her mother, thinking this was some kind of identification technique used in America, did as she was told.

"No, wait," Umi called but her mother's hand was soon covered with multiple red lines of lasers, scanning her skin back and forth until the small cube beeped.

"Help is on its way," it said. She coughed again and the passengers were beginning to look at them. Confused, Umi put her arm around her mother, wondering if there would even be time to take her to the mall or out for noodles. She could feel her throat rising, the tears stinging the backs of her eyes; there was so much between the two lonely women. Her mother rested her head on Umi's shoulder, her frail body rising and falling as she gasped for the air that was all around her.

The train pulled into the next station and when the doors opened, three people in white biohazard suits boarded. They each held what looked like a small camera case in their hands. Umi's stomach turned, suddenly afraid that there was something on the train, something invisible that would soon kill them all. The fear rose as they approached Umi and her mother, and through a speaker on the side of their head covering, they said, "Citizen. You are ill. Please remain seated. You are ill."

Umi looked around, unable to understand what was unfolding in front of her. She twisted her head back and forth, but other than a few people glancing in her direction no one did anything. She put her hand out to one of the uniformed people, lightly, just to get their attention and as she did, they spun around and she saw that the suit was now red where her hand had been. She could not see the eyes of the person in the suit, but the mask tilted downward and back up to her. "Citizen. You are ill. Please remain seated. You are ill."

Her mother's eyes were closed. Umi checked the oxygen and, hearing the rattle in her mother's chest, attached the plastic mask to the tubing. She tugged her mother's disposable face mask down around her chin and placed the oxygen over her nose and mouth. Her mother breathed in then, as deeply as she could which wasn't deep at all, grateful again that she had kept her daughter instead of casting her away as the villagers urged.

"I've got to get my mother to a hospital," Umi said to no one in particular. But the train was still stopped, its doors open. No one got on or off.

"Help is on its way," the smaller of the three suited people said. It was a woman's voice.

She didn't know what was going on and didn't have time to think about it either. What she knew was that her mother must have known she might not survive the flight; Umi hadn't known her condition was this dire. Her mother had hidden it from her just as Umi hid her illness from the world, acknowledging it just long enough to do what was needed before tucking it away to the farthest part of her being once again.

"But I've got to—look, her oxygen is almost out and—". Umi stopped speaking then as two more suited people boarded the train. They each rolled an end of what looked like a tanning bed.

"What is this?" she asked.

"Ma'am," one of the suited people, another woman, said to her mother. "Please take my hand."

Her mother did as she was told, rising to her feet and taking hold of the suited woman's arm. The material crackled and snapped and slowly turned red where her mother held on. It was a darker red than what had been left when Umi had taken her own hand away.

The uited people worked quickly, helping her mother up and over to the contraption. Umi wanted to intervene; who were these people anyway? But it was as though she was paralyzed, haunted by the imagined vision of her father's last moments. Had her mother taken his hand, or had they put his bed outside beyond the tree line so that he could die under the sugi trees he had loved all his life?

She watched as they lay her mother down on the bed, gingerly lifting off the oxygen mask. "Please hold still," the suited woman said to her mother. Her mother did as she was told and Umi watched a red line scan her small, frail body. The people on the train did not look at either of them. Instead they read from their devices and watched the advertisements scroll above. Umi had never seen anything like this before, certainly not on the train, but was unable to put into words the swelling of hope that she felt rising in her chest.

Her mother sat up. Gone was the greyness around her mouth, the shadows of her cheeks and eyes. "Umi?" she asked. "Wakarimsen? Did you do this?"

Umi shook her head, casting her eyes to the woman in the suit. "No, I don't know what's happening. What did you do to her?" she asked.

"She was ill. She is fine now. But you are ill as well. Please, lie down on the table."

"I'm fine," Umi said.

The woman in the suit looked at the hand held device she was carrying. She held it up near Umi's face and pressed a button. "You are ill," she repeated.

For a reason that would forever remain unknown to Umi, she allowed herself to be led to the table. There she lay upon it, her feet parted wide, her hair spilling over the edge. She knew that a red line was scanning her body just as it did her mother's. What she felt was inexplicable. Her mind tried to understand it, but the logical part of her brain was overwhelmed by something else—she felt a wash of calm, the slowing of her heartbeat, the unraveling of the knot in her stomach that she had since…since…she couldn't remember. Before Brianna, before San Francisco, before her father's death and mother's illness. It had always been with her, a grey ball hovering off to the side in her periphery. It had always been with her.

Umi felt herself being helped up—she must've closed her eyes for a moment and as she swung her legs around to get off the contraption, she caught sight of her mother, her hands wringing together as she watched her daughter heal from invisible wounds. And Umi saw her mother was beautiful and well, her face flushed, her breathing steady and unlabored.

"Haha?" Umi asked. "Are you alright? Daijoubu?"

Her mother shrugged, tears glistening in her eyes. "Umi-chan," she said as Umi made her way back to her seat. She picked up her purse so that she could sit down, hearing the bottles of pills rattle in her bag. A feeling swept over her then, an urgent finality: she would no longer need those pills.

The suited people rolled the cart off the train and the doors closed. Some riders looked at them and gave a brief smile, understanding the weight that had been lifted from Umi and her mother. The train lurched forward, gaining speed and took them out of the tunnel into the light of day.

Laura Young is a writer and teacher in the United States. Her work has appeared in *The Lindenwood Review, Cold Creek Review, Parent.co,* and *The Iowa Journal of Cultural Studies.*

Adam-116 reached for his new body.

Michael Stroh

6 word story

44

"The Evolution of African Fantasy and Science Fiction" is the second Call for Papers of Academia Lunare, the non-fiction arm of Luna Press Publishing.

These papers explore the theme through the emergence of African SFF, the forces shaping its development down the ages, and the dangers of expectations. We also examine its effect on literature and portrayals in popular entertainment.

Featuring papers from Peter J. Maurits, Nick Wood, Ezeiyoke Chukwunonso, Polina Levontin and Robert S. Malan.

Release date 07/08/2018

ACADEMIA LUNARE

THE EVOLUTION OF AFRICAN FANTASY AND SCIENCE FICTION

EDITED BY FRANCESCA T BARBINI

"An intriguing and illuminating first collection, chock-full of interesting ideas about the natural world and ourselves."
– Jeff VanderMeer

lost objects

stories by

marian womack

These stories explore place and landscape at different stages of decay, positioning them as fighting grounds for death and renewal. From dystopian Andalusia to Scotland or the Norfolk countryside, they bring together monstrous insects, ghostly lovers, soon-to-be extinct species, unexpected birds, and interstellar explorers, to form a coherent narrative about loss and absence.

"*An intriguing and illuminating first collection, chockfull of interesting ideas about the natural world and ourselves.*"

Jeff VanderMeer

Join us for the Launch Party at Fantasycon 2018!

Splitting Up

Bo Balder

The woman sitting next to us in the café has no control over her splits. She's really rich, since she's clearly got lots of splits, and her companions are frantically trying to deal with them. One moment she sits up straight, sipping delicately from a glass of Bordeaux, the next she rakes her hand through her fabulous coiffure, flicks her fingers, gets a cigarette from an attendant and sucks in smoke like there's no such thing as second hand smoke. If you can't give your splits a lot of time, they can get antsy.

A new expression flits over her face and she starts to cry.

Dana turns away from the spectacle and winks at me. "Jeez. It's pathetic. I wouldn't want to be seen in public like that."

I nod. It's easiest to agree with him, most of the time. He's cute and all, but his standards are really high.

"Actually," I say, "I've been thinking about getting a third split. I made another mistake today at accounting and I can't lose that job."

I work at a gallery. It's good for my contacts, as my real vocation is painting. I've had some small successes. That first sale, anyway.

He makes a face. "Really? Three is a lot to handle at your age." He's like five years older than me. As if he knows. He's got four himself. One to work out his naturally lazy body, one to perform his broker job, one for schmoozing his bosses and contacts after hours, and one he hasn't told me about.

I keep my opinions to myself. That's my job. I smile, I am agreeable, I look up to him. I'm always well-groomed and willing to have sex.

You see, it's not really me getting a third split, it's Bell thinking of getting a fourth split. Remember how I agreed with and lied to Dana? That's my job. I'm the split that Bell calls The Girlfriend.

In my mind, I call her The Bell Formerly Known as Artist. I *think* I've kept that from her. I'm not sure how much privacy I have in my thoughts.

Like Dana, Bell splits off for the things she doesn't really like doing. Like accounting. Like being neat-freak Dana's girlfriend.

Don't ask me how that's working out for her. I'm just a split.

Next morning, or at least I think it's next morning, I wake up late. It must be Sunday. I get a lot of face time in weekends, usually. Dana's body next to me is really warm and I snuggle back in. I feel great. I can't remember the rest of last night, though. If it was the one I remember, Dana was going to the gym and Bell was going to go paint.

She must have changed her mind.

Dana groans and turns over. I turn over as well to keep our knees from clashing. His beard tickles my neck.

His beard? I wake up completely and start turning to check his face out. How much time has passed?

Faster than fast, Bell wakes up too and pushes me out. I manage to hold on to a tiny corner of her mind, enough that I can see out of her eyes, but no more. I'm deaf and can't feel my body. Her body.

Bell snuggles up to the bearded dude. He's like the antithesis to Dana. He's heavily built, heavily muscled, with a beard and long hair, and actually, hair everywhere. So not her type. He could be a stevedore or a construction worker. What is she doing? And if she switched boyfriends in the night or months between my rides, why am I not the one entertaining him?

I'm The Girlfriend. That's what I'm *for.*

I hang on for hours of this silent movie of them snuggling and giggling and having breakfast and more sex. Bell doesn't need me.

I pop up in the middle of a conversation with Dana. I feel like I've literally come up from a deep dive; my heart's beating fast, my ears are ringing, and I feel like I'm going to throw up.

49

"Everything all right?" Dana asks and covers my hand with his big cool one.

Thank god, I can hear and feel again. But I'm still disoriented. Normally I'm like on standby, aware of time passing and what's happening both in and outside of Bell. But now I was totally shut away, in isolation. It's affected me. Dana is more perceptive than I would have thought for noticing.

"I'm feeling a little shaky, not sure why," I tell him.

"It's stressful," he says. "Living like you do, a job that's not your ultimate goal in life, trying to make it in the art world … it's the same for me." And he launches into his usual spiel about how he has it so tough. He's not making it up or anything, he's just kind of oblivious to anybody else's feelings. He thinks a microsecond of his attention is enough and then he can get back to the thrilling subject of himself.

That's different. I feel different about Dana. Has Bell tweaked my parameters or something? It used to make me happy and fulfilled, plying and bending to his needs and wants. Now I feel critical and distanced.

That's not going to work. Dana may be thick-skinned but he notices right away when my attention's not on him. It makes him whiny first, mean second. I apply myself to my plate of spinach and tomato, no dressing. To maintain my perfect girlfriend looks.

The band of my skirt is pinching me. What's Bell been eating? And then I remember the Other Guy. With his not so tight stomach. He's corrupting her, changing her. A wash of angry heat explodes on my face. I must be beet red.

I check Dana to see if he's noticed, but he's staring into his borscht.

"Are you okay yourself?" I ask. "You're so silent."

"It's just – I never know what's up with you."

"What?" That's a horrible allegation. Here I am, working my butt off to be even and pleasant and available, and he says something like that? "What do you mean? When? How?"

"Exactly what I'm talking about. You were the one called me up on Saturday night, asking to meet me after my workout, changing our plans – and then we had a drink and you were so strange, so – wild. Talking about painting and giving up your day job. And then you ran off. And now you're here, smooth as cream, as if nothing happened."

I'm dumbstruck. What the hell? Not only is Bell sleeping with another guy, now she's seeing Dana without putting me on? That's so not in the spirit of splitting. She's undercutting me at my own job.

"Close your mouth," he says, not unkindly.

But he does say it.

We finish the meal in silence. We're going to an opening. A friend of Bell's, a sculptor it says on the invitation. I don't know him or her, which kind of brings it home again how little of Bell's life I'm privy to. Shouldn't I have access to all the memories, to be a better, more lifelike girlfriend?

As we leave the restaurant, I catch sight of the two of us in the plate glass at the entrance. We look good together. We're both tall and slim, me dark and Dana fair. Couldn't be better.

We only have to get Bell in line and this could become a permanent thing. It sounds perfect to me. Why is she sabotaging us?

The taxi ride to the gallery starts out a little tense, but I snuggle under his arm anyway. I sigh a little as I put my head on his shoulders, and he sighs too and kisses my hair. I know without having to check he won't muss my hairdo. I like that about him. It's a lot of work to look like a girlfriend, and Dana takes care not to ruin it.

"We're both tired, I guess," he says. "Do we have to go to this opening?"

"Yeah, it's a small gallery, which might want to show my work. And I know the sculptor from art school."

This latter fact is just that to me, a tidbit Bell has thrown my way without giving me the accompanying memories and feelings. I'm a visual person, and it feels very arid and desolate, but that's how she's been lately.

We get to the gallery, Dana pays the taxi, we enter. It's a shoestring operation, bad neighborhood, bare walls, brick floor. But it's full of excited, smiling people. The opening is a success.

Dana relaxes. He likes to be in the presence of success or money or both.

"Hey, you two lovebirds, finally got here!" crows Miriam, a friend of Bell's. Me. We hug. She air-kisses Dana. "Dana, let me introduce you to Mstislav. You two were at school together, right, Bell?"

I nod.

Bell surges up inside me and takes over. In a last grab at control over her body I make her stagger.

"What is it, baby?' says Dana as he catches me just in time to prevent me stumbling.

"My heel caught on these awful cobbles," Bell says and tries to push me down further. But as she's got to watch Dana, Miriam and the approaching Mstislav, get her bearings, keep her balance; shutting me out completely is just not on.

"Here he is!" Miriam says and pulls forward the furry bear. Other Guy.

Ah. It all becomes clear. Bell is having it off with the sculptor, who can connect to her on an art level that Dana can't. She's having such a good time she doesn't need me anymore. If she needs to split off a personality to deal with Mstislav, it's not going to be me. I was tailored for Dana. This overweight, sloppy, laughing person who makes art, enormous sloppy sculptures that look as gross and bulge as much as he does, would need a completely different type of girlfriend.

What I don't get is why she's still stringing Dana along. That doesn't seem fair.

That's the moment I take my decision. I'm not going to lie down and take it like a good little split. I'm going to make the world more fair. Fair to *me*.

Every time Bell dismisses me, I cling a little harder. At first it seems impossible, the walls of her mind slippery as snot, my hands scrabbling to hold on as I fall down into the deeper well.

But I learn to will handholds into the snot and cling on, my hands ghostly and weak at first, my legs dissolving into nothingness as they flap uselessly below.

I climb back out, hand over hand and hover just below the rim, watching Bell's life. I need to know more than what The Girlfriend knows. I know how to please Dana, how to bend and acquiesce, but not how to do laundry or pay a bill. I have to learn.

I make a nest there, of clean-smelling freshly ironed dishcloths. A haven of neatness and order.

I walk with Bell to the subway, I sell paintings with her, I clean her apartment, buy groceries. I have known echoes of these things before, shadows on the cave wall, but not the real thing. I wonder how Dana could ever have thought he was talking to a real person. Or maybe he fell in love with Bell, and just assumed she was still there when she left me behind to deal with him.

I ride her while she paints. The mixing of colors with medium and varying amount of turpentine is easily understandable. The painting is another matter. I can't feel her arm when she does it, because it really, really matters to her, but I can see the paintings take shape in the white canvas. It doesn't look that hard. I don't think I could do a portrait, but all she does is smear colors, wipe them out, re-smear them, into something resembling children's drawings. I try to gauge her feelings while she's doing it, is it going well or not? But she's impenetrable to me on these moments.

But I'm doing fine. I'm learning fast, I'm growing strong and determined. Soon I'll know enough to be Bell. And she'll be the one howling in the well, shaking up the pillows to make it snow.

I'm content with my progress. Maybe I slacken a little. I fold and stack dishtowels by color graduation, down in my well. I exist, even if she doesn't call on me.

So I'm unprepared that evening. Bell is cooking dinner for me and Dana at his apartment, resentfully I think. I know that emotion well. I get ready to slip into my party dress, my girlfriend persona, ready to smile up at Dana. But Bell doesn't call me.

"Dana," she says. "I asked us to meet here for a reason. I didn't want this to be in a public place."

I can read Dana's face like a book. He freezes. On some level, he knows already. But being Dana, he tries to stave off the inevitable.

"Shh, Bell. Let's not. Let's just enjoy this quiet meal together, okay? I know you've been working hard, and you've been distracted and painting a lot. I understand."

Bell's face heats up. I guess Dana doesn't see any redness, because his earnest, "I-know-what's-the-matter-let-me-solve-it" face remains on. I agree with Bell that he can be dense, but that's not his fault, is it? He's trying to do the right thing. He's trying to be a good boyfriend, I know he is. Bell just has no right.

But I can't stop her.

She pulls her hand back.

"Dana, I'm sorry." Her voice is very level. A sure indication of deep anger. I don't have access to older memories, but I'm guessing her parents trained her not to shout and throw things. "This isn't working, I mean us. It's over. I need more space."

Dana gasps. "I'll give you space," he says. "We don't have to break up! We can change things up, take evenings off, see other people." He swallows.

I love that guy. Look at him with his feelings all naked on his face. Who could not love that? Can't Bell see it's need, not arrogance, that makes him so controlling?

"I'm sorry," she says. "It's me, not you." Yeah, trot out the clichés, sister.

She starts gathering her stuff. Those are my movements, my stuff that my hands have put out, from habit. Packet of Kleenex, because I cry a lot. Lipstick, chapstick, mints.

"Sorry," Bell repeats.

She gets up and leaves. I feel the spring in her step. She's happy. She's relieved! I'm not privy to her plans, but undoubtedly she's hurrying towards her new lover, the fat, ugly sculptor. That's why the dinner was at Dana's place, so she could leave.

On the inside I'm crying, but her eyes won't cooperate and her hands won't offer the Kleenex. I have to bear my grief alone. I love Dana. She's cut off any hope I have of having him and the happy family I long for. She didn't even give me any warning. It's not fair.

Bell's shoes clack on the pavement. They're not hers, really, they're mine. She never wears them except to dates with Dana. He likes to steady my tottering legs. She buttons her coat with trembling fingers. Aha! She is affected by this.

Although she's focused on the pavement, so as not to stumble, I see enough of my surroundings to see it's dark and deserted here. This is the moment.

I surge up through my narrow tunnel, using the new strength I've gathered recently. Out, out, out into the world. I want her brain, her eyes, her feet. I should be the main persona, not stupid Bell who just ruined a perfectly good relationship.

Bell staggers. I grasp for control, it should be now, now that's she's confused. She's stronger than I could have imagined. She lashes back with her fierce will, driving me back into my hellhole. My coffin. I'm desperate, I scrabble, I scratch, I wail, but it's clear it's not enough against her solid sense of possession.

I fall back, exhausted. Bell pushes a strand of hair back from her face and strides towards the subway. I wonder if she even noticed what just took place. Am I so unimportant to her?

I curl up into my neat stacks of just-ironed dishcloths and think.

My eyes are a bit fuzzy and I try to focus on the face of the man in front of me. His voice is vaguely familiar, but I can't place him.

"Are you all right, Miss Liu?" he asks.

Bell sniffs a little and straightens up. That means I can see him better too. He wears a white coat and has unreadable diplomas on the wall behind his back. He's a doctor of some sort. Is Bell's body sick? My body, that is?

"It works like this," the doctor voice says. "We dissolve the walls that we used to separate you and your Separate Temporary Internal Partition, and although at first you might feel a bit disoriented, this feeling will disappear and everything will find its rightful place again. I like to compare it with starting to wear bifocal glasses. At first there can be some swimmy vision and headaches, but once the brain gets used to the bifocals, the world looks quite normal again."

The doctor smiles widely. Bell's a pretty girl. The thing is, his teeth look like tombstones. Like he should be named Grandmother and be in bed, waiting for his granddaughter to bring him cookies.

Bell shifts in her seat. "But. Can't you just delete that part? I put things in there that I don't need any more. I'm fine without them, better than I've ever been."

She stares hopefully at the doc, unaware, it seems, of me screaming in the background and tearing my lovely folded towels in half. Cut me out? What the hell?

The doctor staples his fingers. The lecher is gone, the professional is back. "Even if we could excise part of your brain, your personality, we wouldn't. A human being needs his or her faults, or less desirable characteristics to be whole."

Bell snorts. "That's so, so, judgmental. Aren't I the boss of my own brain?"

"You *are* your own brain, Ms. Bell. That means you can't look at it and say I like this piece but not that piece. Because you can never look at yourself objectively."

Bell opens her mouth.

The doctor waves whatever she's going to say away. "I'm saying no. I'll happily reintegrate you and your split, but nothing you are thinking of right now is possible or wise."

"All right," Bell says. "I knew that. You know, just tried on the off chance. I just don't like to have her floating around in my head. How do I know she won't take me over?"

"Ha ha ha. That is impossible. She is you. If you don't like her, you will just have to deal with her the way you deal with all the habits and traits you're less proud of. Like biting nails."

Bell sits on her hands. I never bite our nails, but I'm not around enough to change her habits.

"If you dislike that part of yourself that much, you can just keep the division," the doctor suggests.

"Too expensive," Bell says. "Just do it."

The doctor's assistant leads her to the chair, where they shave bits of her hair and put on a net full of electrodes to her skull.

I'm stacking dish towels like mad. This is an opportunity. But what kind? I need to have my stuff in order. I don't want to be dispersed. I gather my towels to me and hold on tight.

There's a series of sharp green flashes, changing in rhythm. It stirs a faint memory. I know I must have gone through something like this before, my birth, but like most babies, I have no conscious memories of it.

I gather myself into one final screaming surge upward, flinging dishtowels behind, me like exhaust gases from a jet.

I'm in an empty house. Light pours in through enormous overhead windows. It's like an idealized version of a painter's studio. So much larger than Bell's in real life. It's full of wall-sized canvases, but unlike the floorboards and the paint splatters I can't get those into focus.

I don't know what this means, but I know I need to take possession of it. My arms are full of dishtowels, ironed and folded and stacked to perfection. I have to let them go if I am to take anything else.

I don't want to. They smell so good, of cleanness and sunshine and having been ironed. That scorched linen smell. They look so pretty and comforting, all neat and aligned just so.

But I want Bell's life more. I don't want to dissolve into her untidy life without Dana. It should be mine.

I set down the towels on the cleanest surface I can find. It's like a murder scene if blood had rainbow colors. I cringe when I let go of my towels. I feel naked and empty.

How to take this room? I touch everything I can, biting away the horror of all these dirty surfaces. If I am to be a painter, I have to be able to touch paint and crusty brushes and paint tubes. I crawl over the floor, hug the easels, sniff the blank canvases. I can't get any closer to the finished paintings, and I can't get them into focus. But that's fine. I hope. The room is mine.

Now the rest of the house.

That's easier, because it's cleaner. I find the bedroom, the living room, the bathroom. There are locked doors as well. Such a huge place. If only Bell's apartment was more like this.

There are photographs artfully arranged on the wall behind the sofa. They are horrible quality, blurred to invisibility. Bell is still trying to hide stuff from me. The bookcase is full of empty books, which is weird, but who cares. I'm not a big reader, I don't think.

I've gone through all the rooms. I own the house. Now, I think, I should go outside and face the world. Not literally. I know this is a metaphor of some kind. What I need to do is open the eyes and make the body sit up. No more fraidy cat, just go and do it.

I stride to the front door and fling it open.

The light is so bright that my eyes tear up.

"Sorry, Ms. Liu, that should have been dimmed already. How are you feeling?"

I try to sit up. Cool hands help me. Blink blink. I have the body, I have the eyes. I smile at the doctor, who flickers the tombstones at me. Dana has much better teeth than that. I could never kiss these.

The doctor drones to me, but I'm not really paying attention. They help me into a wheelchair, put my bag into my lap, push me to a recovery area with soothing music and soft light.

I'm in the real world. No Bell. I won, I won, I won! I guess I never thought I would. But I have to be careful. The staff can't suspect. I shall be Bell to perfection.

I try to keep up polite conversation, but I can't really concentrate on anybody but myself. I wiggle my toes and my fingers. I discover I can even wiggle my ears. Why did Bell bother to learn that? After an hour of this, they let me out.

I step out onto the pavement, dressed in Bell's casual clothes – grungier than I like – and breathe deeply. I get a noseful of engine fuel and river whiff. Has my sense of smell improved? Did Bell not give me the full array of senses when she made me? I guess it's not important.

I take the subway home and walk up the three flights of stairs to Bell's apartment. It's cramped and messy, so unlike the grand rooms of her mind. I'll be making some changes here.

I check to see what day it is. Odd, that I don't know that already. I can learn to anchor myself in time and place more, it's just that I never had to. It's a Thursday, so probably Bell got the day off for her procedure. I feel fine, though, so what should I do with my day of freedom? I don't want to call Mstislav. I don't even know his phone number. I check Bell's phone. She doesn't have a Mstislav, but maybe it's under M? I should know these things. I'm not going to let it faze me.I shall paint. That's the proper, Bell way to use free time.

I put on her painting gear. The coverall is stiff with old, dry paint. I'm going to have it laundered as soon as possible. Being a painter is no excuse for sloppiness.

The small workspace is light, but cluttered. I managed to restrain myself from cleaning up. I'm Bell now. I should act like her. Paint first, clean later. Never, in Bell's case, but later in the new Bell. Bell Superior. Bell Better.

I snigger to myself. I'm an artist, I can be weird.

I find a clean, already prepared canvas and put it on an easel. I mix up some paints. With a lot of turpentine for the first layer, I know that. I watched Bell.

So. Broad brush, for a light, sketched in layer. That's how Bell does it. I lift the brush, saturated with the thin paint, ready for the first stroke. Where shall I put it?

No inspiration comes.

That's fine. Sometimes Bell putters around a bit first, looks at other paintings. I do that. I putter. I straighten a few things. It's fun, but I need to get back to painting.

Maybe a nice, firm, diagonal line? I execute it. It doesn't look like Bell's first layer yet. Maybe another one. No. Another color then?

The hours stretch. I wipe the canvas clean again and again, which I can do because oils don't dry that fast, not without medium. Why isn't this working? Where does inspiration come from, anyway?

Bell's mind gives no answer. I don't even know how she learned to paint. That's odd that I have no memories of that. I know for a fact that Bell went to art school. That she always doodled in class, from kindergarten on.

No memories come.

Maybe her parents gave her the inborn talent? Or her experiences shaped her?

Nothing comes. A feeling of dread creeps up over my spine. This can't be true.

I stalk out of the workroom and go find Bell's linen closet. She must have dish towels.

She has. Three. I find them flung willy-nilly around her kitchen, all dirty and creased. I gather them to me anyway. I lay them out, press them as flat as they get, fold them neatly and balance them on my palms.

There. Dishtowels at the ready.

Where does inspiration come from? Where is the rest of Bell?

I remember the closed rooms in the apartment of Bell's mind. The blurred photographs of her family, the invisible paintings.

It doesn't help.

The skylight overhead darkens as I sit and hug my stinky dishtowels.

Bo Bolder is the first Dutch author to have been published in *Clarkesworld* and *F&SF*. Her short fiction has also appeared in *Escape Pod*, *Nature* and other places. Her sf novel 'The Wan' was published by Pink Narcissus Press. Visit her website: www.boukjebalder.nl

Starfield
science fiction by Scottish writers

Edited by
Duncan Lunan

A loving re-creation of a classic collection of Scottish science fiction.

Published by Shoreline of Infinity

Publications
paperback, 240pp £11.95
ISBN 978-1-9997002-2-5

Stories and poems by

Angus MacVicar

Chris Boyce

David John Lee

Naomi Mitchison

Janice Galloway

Louise Turner

Angus McAllister

Edwin Morgan

Elsie Donald

William King

David Crooks

alburt plethora

Richard Hammersley

Alasdair Gray

Donald Malcolm

Duncan Lunan

Archie Roy

Cover: Sydney Jordan

www.shorelineofinfinity.com

Goodnight Rosemarinus

Caroline Grebbell

The Observer spoke.

"Continue."

The single line of a circle disintegrated as twelve opalescent charge spheres split apart.

"Polygon. Three vertices. Closed."

The Observer scanned for irregularities or flickers of noncompliance, rebellious traits so indicative of the species. It stood motionless and without shadow, its dark casing sucking the light from the sub-terra viewing chamber. Hewn from gabbro and lined on one side by a thick wall of Espejan glass, the facility sat in the depths of what was once the Eurasian Basin. A loosely defined arena had been ripped from the heart of the kelp forests. Ribboned lines of sickly fronds, fluttering like blackened lace around the edges of the barren ocean floor.

The Observer's gaze shifted and locked. One sphere traversed too rapidly. It swerved, catching the edge of another causing both to lose their place within the configuration. In the space of a human heartbeat two forms became visible, their skins pulsing with intermittent light. Adults, limbs wasted and thin, each one cradling a charge sphere within folded arms. The Observer was obdurate, it did not hesitate.

"Thri. Acht."

The beings looked to each other and opened their arms wide as their charge spheres shattered and their bodies disintegrated within jagged flares of incandescence.

"Resume".

Replacement spheres dropped into view, followed immediately by those chosen to carry them. The figures flickered, then faded to be one with the ocean while the smooth sided weapons remained, falling in line with the others.

"What did he tell you?" The Observer did not turn to address its prisoner.

A young female stood at the opposite side of the chamber, her long, fine-boned hands hanging loose, the web roughly folded, pinned through with a shard of metal. She could see her reflection in the curve of The Observer's head-part.

"You haven't always been an Observer." The female turned exposing streaks of brown pin-head spores which had blossomed across the surface of her flesh. "Are you of the manumit, the unbound?"

The Observer continued to survey the charge spheres as they grouped to form a triangle. Its body was blackened and hardened by the fumes of the Audex mines and it had the short rigid feet of a rock dweller.

"A warning. The Patience of The Opraesent is finite."

"Well, can I speak to them?" She was irritated, the informant had guaranteed an audience with the protector.

The Observer turned. It spoke in a calm, flat way, reiterating a point already made.

"The Opraesent has no interest in you."

The female pointed to The Observer's chest-part, to the row of glistening pips positioned above the place a heart might sit.

"Only in the black Audax." She mocked. "You're not so different to the ones you assume to be our gods."

The Observer's head-part shifted slightly. "Rosemary. That is your given name?"

"May I have some water?"

"Rosemary. Rosemarinus, from the sea."

When first presented, The Observer had examined the prisoner thoroughly, as if having only seen her type for the first time. This one was unusual, smaller than the others, with hair the hue of rusted iron, skin pale and marked with swathes of mottled discolouration. Rosemary hooked her hands beneath the hem of her tunic and raised the fabric to the edge of her jaw. The pain of the pinning shot through her arms and across her chest where rows of frail gills sat shrunken and brittle. She placed a ruined hand on her belly and the skin flickered coral before returning to the lacklustre grey she had become. Rosemary spoke without raising her eyes. She spoke softly.

"We are all from the water. From the Saccorhytus, trapped for millennia between two grains of sand, to the sapiens who wallowed stupidly in their polymer age. The Atavist, the Éclairé. We are all from the water."

Rosemary looked to the ocean and felt the echoes of her words returned to her. She staggered, her

balance for standing weakened, unsteady on soft feet hardened by the rough baked earth of the lower levels. She focussed on a corner of the chamber, at the point where walls met in darkness. There were no corners in her world.

"You will die soon if you do not hydrate." The Observer said. "Tell me what they told you and I will unpin you. I will move you to Aquatic where you will sleep immersed. Your mind will clear to the truth. Your wounds will heal and in the new dawn you will be reunited with your father."

"And my mother?"

"What did they tell you?"

A tear fell to the floor, a reminder of what Rosemary had been and what she still was. She could not afford such a loss. "They said you command them, as the sapiens did the Delphinidae."

"Command?"

"To spread your ruin."

"Is that what they told you?"

With a sweep of its arm The Observer directed Rosemary to cross the chamber. It raised a slim metal finger and pointed out towards the charge spheres.

"Unu."

A light flashed within the water and a figure appeared and as the sphere shattered it glimmered and was gone.

"The ruin is yours Rosemary. It is your silence that destroys them."

Rosemary felt the chill of their bodies. She could hear them clearly now but their pitiful cries at the touch of her gaze had altered. They signalled. They could see her and they were ready.

"Vier."

A flame consumed another.

"End this now." Rosemary rested her forehead against the glass but her eyes remained open and bright.

"Kuus."

She took a breath, her stomach soured, her muscles tight with anticipation.

"They told us nothing we did not already know. You arrived. You misled us. You blast apart our shelters. You poison us. You ravage our world for the Audax." Rosemary paused. "That's all they said. Please, I am of no further use to you."

The air in the chamber grew heavy.

"You are lying Rosemary." The Observer turned again to the spheres as Rosemary took a step towards him. She appeared hesitant.

"They told me to come, that I could talk to The Opraesent. That it would let me see them. My father. My mother."

The Observer did not betray its response.

Rosemary leant her aching spine against the wall. She took one hand in the other and started to ease her fingers apart. She pressed gently at the fine bones which felt frail as avian. She uncurled them, a slow tearing as the pins pulled through the tender folds. The Observer spoke.

"There is nowhere for you to go, Rosemary."

Rosemary raised her hands in tattered fans to flatten them against the glass, curves of tortured cartilage lit by the ocean.

"Sceft."

A ragged flash and another gone.

"Teog."

Another.

Rosemary looked to The Observer, a smile reflected in its head-part. Beyond her the soft fog of the water swirled and twisted and the five remaining spheres dropped from sight. Rosemary spoke, her tenor steely.

"You look tired Observer, why don't you sleep, it will clear your mind to the truth."

She dropped her head back and pressed her hands harder against the glass as her mouth fell open and her lungs filled with hot loathsome air.

"Rosemary." The Observer did not move to contain her, its words crushed by the silence which now filled the chamber. "End this now."

Five forms became visible at the window, their restored colours flickered and flashed as they moved forward together to lay their hands on the glass. They tipped back their heads and opened their mouths to resound the command of their young deliverer.

"Your parents are dead."

Rosemary tilted her head to one side, eyes flooded with bioluminescence. She smiled at The Observer, her lips parted, soft and full and heavy with salt.

"I know."

Beneath the hands the glass snapped to filigree and a fat bead of sea water squeezed through to settle on Rosemary's skin before bursting to a glistening trail. Then another, and another and as the fissures leapt across the glass Rosemary's arms were soaked, then her body, her legs, her lovely face shining as bright as the silver scales of Scombridae armour. The Observer did not move. It did not pull at Rosemary or speak her name but only watched as the Espejan glass exploded into and across the chamber. The Observer rose and dropped, powerless against the surge and heft of the ocean. Its blackened form sank to the earth where it lay watching as many arms reached out to Rosemary to take her and wrap her within them, webbed hands and feet flared wide to protect her as she crashed against the walls of the chamber.

The world stilled and Rosemary glided silently above The Observer as the waters equalled. She peered down at the incapable carapace rocking gently as a baby's cot beneath her.

"Goodnight Observer." Her skin shimmered as she prepared to leave. Sleep well."

Rosemary flicked her body to pass through the portal which was once a wall, and Rosemarinus vanished with her kind into the icy freedom of a cherished world.

Caroline Grebbell writes speculative and graphic fiction, and was co-guest editor for *Shoreline of Infinity 11*. She is a BSFA nominee and in a parallel universe is employed as an art director in tv/film.
www.carolinegrebbell.co.uk @Grebbell

We Have a Winner –

Jimmy McGregor

After much consideration, our art team has chosen a winner of our Goodnight Rosemarinus illustration competition. We had a number of very good images submitted but all agreed that Jimmy McGregor's illustration was the best depiction of the story, a good balance of drawing skill and sensitivity to the written work.

Story author Caroline Grebbell summed up the judges' decision. "I thought Jimmy McGregor's illustration was an excellent interpretation of my story.

"Rosemarinus, strengthened by her foreground positioning, is clearly an empowered female. She has turned her back on her oppressor and her focussed gaze stares directly out of the page so engaging the reader. In the background, illuminated by its own light, stands The Observer. The lines of its carapace echo those of Rosemarinus, but its metal hands are powerless to act against her.

"When I look at this illustration I feel that I want to know more about these characters. I want to read the story."

Jimmy McGregor lives in Hawick, in the Borders of Scotland.

The runners-up are **Emma Howitt** from Melton Mowbray, England and **Eve Murray** from Edinburgh.

Thanks to the winners and to all who entered.

Quicksilver Delivery. Tomorrow's message sent yesterday.

Gregg Chamberlain

71

Cast In the Same Mould

Tim Major

Art: Jessica Good

It was a clear, bright day in the month that the first Martian settlers had dubbed May. With an eye on the incline that led to the dry docks, Liss Crowther took the strap attached to the pram handle and twisted it around her wrist.

"He wailed the whole journey," she said, indicating Rory, asleep in the pram. "I can't tell you how frustrating it is that he looks so angelic now. I could barely concentrate."

Rory had begun grizzling immediately after they had dropped his older sister at school. Hannah had been equally disgruntled at her abandonment and her complaints had still been audible as Liss wheeled the pram back to the carriage pod. In truth, her son had quieted as the carriage had descended, whipping Martian dust as it approached the glittering lights that surrounded the docks. It was a rare sight, three crawler bases returning to dock at once. Perhaps even an infant could recognise the sense of occasion.

Ivan Follett ignored her complaint. "Should get reins for this one," he said. His arm pulled straight as he grasped at the collar of his seven-year-old daughter, Tallie. The girl's neck craned awkwardly to peer up at the huge vehicle resting in the dry dock, overshadowing them.

Liss remembered Ivan's detachment from other events that their respective children had attended. She resented her wife's encouragement to socialise, to mend fences. In her opinion, Hannah had been justified in lashing out at Tallie during the swimming gala. The Follett girl had gripped her daughter's heel in the qualifier, preventing her from pulling ahead. After the race Tallie had only smirked while Hannah cried.

"Hannah talks of nothing but crawlers at the moment," Liss said. "Have you seen their classroom recently? The walls are crammed full of pictures of the bases being constructed. Cross-sections, tools, papier-mâché models, you name it."

She felt a flicker of annoyance that Ivan seemed to bear no guilt in removing his daughter from school for the day. Not only did it foil her plan to discuss the girls' behaviour openly, it represented another point of difference between them. Tonight, Hannah would punish both Liss and her other mother, Marian. Tantrums before bed.

"This one's Tharsis Caraway," Tallie said, pointing up to the hull that hung above them. "The others are Cowslip and Catchfly, they must be hidden behind. Caraway's my favourite, it's got six carriage-pads and its back is painted a sort of green. We ate caraway pudding in class yesterday."

"There – what did I tell you?" Liss said to Ivan. She shielded her eyes to look up at Tharsis Caraway. The scale of these older crawlers seemed too great for her to fully appreciate their size. Tall struts supported the upended bell of the vehicle. The hull curved out from a slender lower end, modelled around the contours of an Earth water-ship, where wheels and tracks had now retracted into its smooth surface. The crawler blocked the bloom-halo sun that refracted through the protective dome far overhead. Liss shivered.

It ought to feel familiar. Wasn't her own city, Tharsis Foxglove, constructed around a central base just like it? But without the surrounding residential domes and towers, this limbless crawler seemed a natural phenomenon, an inverted mountain.

"We'd better let her get on," Ivan said as Tallie yanked at his arm.

It being a school day, the queue at the ticket booth was short. Ivan paid for all four of them in a manner that Liss interpreted as a challenge rather than a favour. She smiled her thanks and wrestled the pram onto the narrow lift. As the mechanism stirred into motion, so did Rory. He smacked his lips for a few moments, then turned his head and drifted off to sleep again.

Once they reached the deck, Liss spun slowly to orient herself. The flat deck was vast and almost featureless, gunmetal grey. A network of rips and scrapes lined its surface: when in motion, the crawler would be enveloped in dust. She had once been told that the vortex created by the forward movement of a crawler could create localised dust storms that would then wander the surface of Mars in its wake, hollow ghosts of the huge vehicle.

She shielded her eyes to make out figures further along the deck. Scattered family groups faced the city, Foxglove, children squinting to identify their houses and cul-de-sac pods. With each group stood a taller, aloof figure, who must be an aye-aye. In the opposite direction the other two crawlers, Cowslip and Catchfly, appeared from this altitude sleek and low, like kneeling dogs. Their wheels and caterpillar tracks still supported them; they would not come fully into the dry docks. The arrival of these crawlers at the docks represented their single maintenance session, precisely halfway through their lifespan, before they were sent on their way again. Within weeks they would once again trundle the Tharsis dust, trawling for muck and data, hoovering up the loose regolith to process into breathable gas for the pod-dwellers. At the end of their four-year tours of duty they would begin the search for ideal locations for settlement. Once found, they would crouch and bury themselves into the rock, waiting for human operators to add the pods and domes to transform their utilitarian structures into cities that would grow like spiderwebs from newly-static centres.

In contrast, Tharsis Caraway's journey had ended. It had returned to dry dock and its aging facilities had been deemed unsuitable to be a city catalyst, therefore it had failed and would be retired.

"Where does the driver sit?" Ivan asked.

Tallie snorted. "Silly daddy. There's nobody driving. It's all romantic."

"You mean automatic," Ivan said. He turned to Liss. "Seriously though, is the route-finding at hardware level, or are there actual aye-aye drivers?"

A surprisingly coherent question from somebody that Liss had, intellectually speaking, already written off. She was used to fielding questions about robots, referred to as 'aye-ayes' by most people. Since completing her doctorate on the learning abilities of the machines, and being deemed articulate and presentable by the media, she had been in demand whenever aye-ayes were the topic for discussion on talk shows. At least, until she had taken maternity leave after the birth of their second child.

"The short answer is hardware. It's different tech entirely," she said. "Turns out that while using human templates for aye-aye brain processes is a smart idea, it's hopeless for specialised equipment. A crawler base with human-like intelligence just meanders around in circles. It's agonising. Better to give it clearly defined parameters. Find a dust-bowl with a twenty-degree incline, sheltered from western winds, within carriage-range of city X. Once found, drill the substrate for traces of anything useable. Rinse and repeat. That sort of thing."

Ivan nodded, but his attention had diverted again. Tallie rushed along the length of the deck to a single silver door that broke up its blank expanse. Liss heaved the pram to follow. Beside the door stood an aye-aye dressed in a dark uniform, complete with peaked cap. Some effort had been put into making it appear more human; even the control stems at the end of its arms were hidden by the sleeves of its outfit. As they drew closer she saw that, rather than the usual blank surface, its smooth face bore crayon-scrawled circular eyes and a lopsided, smiling mouth.

Ivan recoiled. "Well, that's the creepiest thing I've seen for a while." He bent low to see beneath the peaked cap. "Hey. You know you've got scribble on your face?"

The aye-aye twitched into motion. Its arms spread. "Decorate your own tour guide. Three pm at the engineer's cabin. Fun for children." It combined a bow with the motion of pulling open the heavy, scratched door.

"Let's give that a miss," Ivan said as they entered.

Inside, the tour guide aye-aye followed them along the dim, inclined corridor into a wider oval area with five exits.

"From here you can access all of the areas used by the human crew," the aye-aye said. "Bunkhouse, canteen, leisure area, monitor station."

"Leisure!" Tallie said immediately. "Dad, they've got pinball."

Ivan nodded, genuinely impressed.

The leisure area was disappointingly small, combining the functions of lounge and gym. Liss reminded herself that these older crawlers had a crew of only a handful of humans, with aye-ayes performing most of the day-to-day functions.

Confusingly, two decommissioned aye-ayes in fixed positions had been dressed in human crew uniforms. One slumped inert on a sofa, facing a screen. The other hung from monkey bars at the dark rear of the room.

Tallie groaned. The pinball machine was jammed.

Another waxwork aye-aye stood stock-still in a bunkhouse room, leaning as if about to climb into bed.

"They've really nailed the family-friendly tone," Ivan said.

Liss glanced at the tour guide. Despite her training, she wondered whether it felt some form of discomfort, witnessing other robots locked in paralysis. The aye-aye turned, displaying its childish, crooked smile.

"I'm bored," Tallie said.

Ivan, too, looked dejected. They were very alike, father and daughter. Impatient and bordering on selfish. Ivan had no right to look perturbed — hadn't it been his idea to meet here? Liss was the one struggling with a pram. She had told him that this wasn't a suitable venue.

"How about the kitchens?" Ivan said. "I'm starving."

"The food has been removed," the aye-aye said. "Come, see the monitoring station."

But both Ivan and Tallie dismissed the remaining crew rooms. They clomped together along the gantry towards an area lit by glowing red lamps. When Liss arrived, grunting with the exertion of the pram wheels juddering against the rough floor, Tallie stood before a glass cubicle containing a bulky engineer's suit. The light made shifting red chevrons on its curved visor.

"Can I try it on?" she said, addressing the aye-aye.

The aye-aye bent low. Its graffiti smile appeared to flicker, a trick of the light. Acting on instinct, Liss placed a protective hand on Tallie's shoulder.

"This is a very old suit," the aye-aye said. "And will never be worn again. Tharsis Caraway is dead."

As Liss pulled Tallie away, the girl said, "Then it's stupid. I want to see the sandpit."

Liss looked to Ivan for confirmation, but he stood in silence before the red-lit suit, no doubt lost in his own boyhood daydreams. He trailed along, looking over his shoulder as the group headed to the rear of the crawler. The pram wheels bumped noisily on the floor gratings.

The corridor ended at a wide, concave window, its lower edge rimmed with buttons and displays. Through the window, spinning red lamps illuminated enormous hillocks of sand that seemed to go on for miles. Liss peered through the dust-scratched plastic, trying to determine the point where the hillocks ended and the vertical drop to the lower floors of the crawler base began.

"So, with the pinball machine out of operation, this must be where the spacemen play when they're off-duty?" Ivan said.

"No," the aye-aye said.

"I was being facetious."

The aye-aye cocked its head. "When Tharsis Caraway is in motion, the dust chamber acts as a temporary receptacle. As well as a proportion of the regolith being filtered and processed, the vortex created by the upward motion of particles sucked through the lower-front portal and travelling at high speed to this chamber at the rear contributes to the momentum of the base." It paused. "Was. Contributed."

Liss frowned. The aye-aye appeared to be struggling to process Caraway's retirement. A glitch, or grief?

"I want to play in the sandpit," Tallie said.

To Liss's surprise, Ivan smiled and nodded.

"You cannot enter the chamber," the aye-aye said.

Ivan pushed forwards to the door beside the curved window. At a push of a button, it slid open.

"No wearing of suits, no playing in the sand," Ivan said. "What kind of tour is this? Coming, Liss?"

Dumbstruck, Liss shook her head.

"Stay near the door, Tallie," Ivan called as his daughter danced into the chamber. The aye-aye fidgeted beside him in the doorway, its body language as nervous as Ivan's was relaxed.

Liss placed both hands on the curved window. Tallie whooped, drawing sand up in handfuls and flinging it into the air. She dug deep with her fingers. She made angel shapes in the dust.

Liss turned at a splutter from behind. Rory's eyes had opened wide. They gazed at each other for a few silent seconds in which the boy seemed far older and more experienced than his eight months. Then his mouth crumpled and he began to wail.

She sighed. "Excuse me?" she said, tapping the aye-aye's arm. "Is there somewhere private nearby? My son needs feeding."

The tour guide directed her to a nearby cabin, thankfully without an aye-aye occupant. Though small, its interior had been decorated tastefully. Pale, leaf-patterned wallpaper, minimalist furniture, the complete works of Jules Verne. Even with the door closed Liss could hear Tallie's delighted calls.

Rory fed quietly, although Liss knew that, once finished, he would be ready to play. He would be alarmed by the darkness of the crawler base and her tour would come to an abrupt end.

Tallie's muted whoops became more insistent. What was she saying?

She finished up quickly. Rory grumbled complaints. She held him close, using the pram to force open the door.

Her eyes ached as they adjusted again to the darkness. At the end of the corridor, the tour guide stood with its back to her. The door to the dust chamber wheezed as it closed.

She cleared her throat. "Could you let me know which way my friends went?"

The aye-aye remained motionless. Had it not heard her?

She turned at a sound from behind. Ivan strode down the corridor, from the direction of the oval area where they had seen the engineer's suit in its cubicle.

"Couldn't resist taking another look," he said. "I can't tell you how much I want to try that thing on." He prodded at the aye-aye. "Hey, buster. Come on, if we can play in the sand, surely you can crack open the spaceman costumes?"

His pace slowed as he noticed the closed door to the dust chamber. "Where's Tallie?"

Discreetly, the aye-aye reached out to push a single button on the control panel.

Liss turned to look into the dust chamber. Inside, Tallie turned, too. The look on her face was somewhere between curiosity and horror. The girl held her arm outstretched, pointing to the lumpy ground.

The floor grilles beneath Liss's feet rattled.

"No. No!" She thumped the aye-aye's arm. "Turn it off!"

The aye-aye gazed through the window, impassive, as if lost in thought.

Liss held her son too tight to her chest. She hammered on the control panel beneath the window. She sensed Ivan behind her, unmoving.

Fans buried deep beneath the sand dunes stirred into motion. Rory's burbling became a howl.

Ivan pressed himself against the concave window as sand danced upwards from the shaft at the far end of the huge chamber. Reddish streams swung through the airspace, whirling towards the window as corkscrew currents. Within seconds, Tallie disappeared behind a veil of shifting dust.

The aye-aye turned, its scribbled smile benign as it watched Ivan's fists thump against the plastic.

"Stop. Back up," Liss said.

The aye-aye tilted its head, not understanding the command. Its segmented neck snagged against the sculpted restraints of the holding chair.

"Repeat," Liss said.

"I have no explanation for my actions," the aye-aye said.

Liss exchanged glances with the technician, Jay, who sat beside her. He shrugged.

"What about the girl?" she said, addressing the aye-aye again.

"She was inside the chamber. A restricted area."

"That's not the point, and you know it."

"I know it."

Liss resettled herself in her seat. "Another question. Why did the fans start?"

"A routine test to check the flow of the sand. Even in dry dock, the sand must be circulated to avoid corrosion."

Once again, the aye-aye seemed in denial about the future of Tharsis Caraway. Corrosion or no corrosion, the crawler had been scheduled for the scrapheap. And since the incident that morning, it wouldn't even fulfil its final purpose of educating visitors. The whole vehicle had been put in lockdown immediately after the incident had been reported.

"You killed a girl. Your actions killed a girl named Talia Follett."

The aye-aye flinched. Its crayon eyes and mouth had been rubbed off since it had been brought to the holding cell, by whoever had removed its tour guide outfit. But even without facial features, its body language suggested anxiety. "The dust chamber is restricted."

Liss sighed. She was getting nowhere and they had been fools for bringing her in. For all her research, what did she really know? After decades of updates and adjustments, the protocols determining aye-aye behaviour had become as labyrinthine as humans' own.

"For the record," she said to the aye-aye, "Tell me your shell and OS history."

Liss interpreted reluctance in its pause before speaking. "I am A-I-eight-five-five. My shell was cast in Tharsis Primrose, theta-one-five batch—"

"The same batch as Caraway itself?"

Ai855 nodded as best it could, given the neck restraints.

Nothing unusual there. Liss waved a hand for it to continue.

"I run on operating system three-one-six-zero-zero-two, developed on Earth. My template was Doctor Caspar Edberg."

All in order, then. Edberg had been one of the founding fathers of the aye-aye constitution, unimpeachable. She stood and motioned for Jay to follow her into the corridor.

"It defies explanation," the technician said. "There's no way it should have been able to put a child in harm's way, let alone cause her death. Primacy of human life, and all that. It's hard-coded."

"So this whole thing didn't happen, then?"

Jay frowned and shrugged again. That was the problem with the new aye-aye techs. No imagination. They were little more than robots themselves.

But wasn't he right? Countless tests had been conducted during the development of the OS for aye-ayes. In lab conditions, puppies, cadavers and robots placed under threat were ignored by aye-ayes, in favour of human protection, without fail.

So there must be another explanation.

Liss broke the news to Hannah in the carriage on the way home from school. Her daughter took it well, in the sense that she absorbed the information, asked a single question – "Was Tallie still angry at me?" – then lapsed into thoughtful silence. Liss filled the evening with activities and games, side-stepping queries about a visit to the dry docks. She allowed Hannah to feed Rory synthetic avocado.

After dinner she watched the two children at play in the conservatory. Rory's efforts to crawl were beginning to bear fruit. As Hannah helped him plant one hand after another on the linoleum, the boy turned to face Liss. His eyes shone, triumph mixed with the knowledge that he was watched and loved. She knew that look. When her wife, Marian, was most satisfied with work or some other achievement, she wore the exact same expression. Rory was young enough to sometimes seem a tiny facsimile of Marian, a baseline template to be adjusted and extruded through his own life experiences. Liss found the thought comforting, that he and Marian might have been cast in the same mould.

Her attention drifted from the children to the view through the conservatory window. The house stood on the outskirts of Tharsis Foxglove, facing the shallow industrial lands, the sand-sculpting factories and the dry docks.

A theory began to crystallise in her mind. She closed her eyes and the pink, sunlit veins of her eyelids became slender threads intertwining.

She reached for the phone.

Liss's demands to have Tharsis Caraway's dust chamber emptied met with initial refusals. Tallie's mangled body had been easy to extract; Caraway was already set to be junked, and Ai855 could simply be added to the furnace, after all. Liss pulled in favours from her research mentors with links to Sandcastle's crawler-tech departments. The academics threatened a PR disaster.

So that's how they found the thing.

News of the discovery travelled fast. The first media reports described it as a crab, later ones as a sort of land-dwelling ray fish. Small enough to pass through Caraway's suction portal, tough enough to withstand being walloped around within its dust chamber. A secretive investigation released only one official photo, blurry and indistinct.

Liss wasn't asked to appear on talk shows to discuss her experience. Perhaps her being a specialist in aye-aye behaviour complicated her status as a witness. Ivan popped up regularly, though, having jacked in his job at one of the smaller sand-sculpting forges. He had not called Liss since the visit to the dry docks, and she had not pursued him either. On the talk shows he, too, recalled seeing his daughter point down to the sand before she was swallowed up. Tallie became at once a pioneer and a martyr, the discoverer of native life on Mars. The details of her death became overlooked.

Liss watched the city of Tharsis Fuchsia grow to fill the carriage window. Far smaller than Foxglove, Fuchsia retained a contented calm, the quiet smugness of wealth. A single tower rose to meet the vehicle, spindly and remote from the beetle carapace of the city centre. The carriage docked in silence. She presented her credentials to the cockpit scanner, which interfaced with the host system.

As she stepped onto the plush carpet, she felt an abrupt and profound longing for her family. The hotel-like surroundings in which she found herself seemed a world from the suburban bustle of her own cul-de-sac. When she returned to Foxglove, she and Marian would take the children swimming.

The door to the apartment swung open as she entered. The lighting, though softer, was as dim as the corridors of Caraway.

"Doctor Edberg?" Her voice echoed oddly. For the first time, she noticed that the walls were bare girders and sculpted concrete, an industrial style at odds with the baroque exterior of the tower.

A silhouetted figure sat before a long window. Liss crept around him, unsure whether he might be asleep.

"Sit down." His voice was little more than a croak.

She perched on the tip of a nearby sofa. Despite the occasion, she felt nervous at meeting such an eminent scientist, so familiar from her research texts.

Dr Edberg occupied a bath chair, an incongruous period feature in these plain surroundings. Brown-filtered sunlight threw into relief the deep creases in his forehead and cheeks.

"Thank you for agreeing to see me," Liss said. More favours. She would spend the rest of her career in the debt of academic higher-ups.

If Dr Edberg felt any pleasure in the pension rewards and immunity that Liss's recent activities had granted him, he didn't show it.

"I get few visitors." The way he said it, this might have be either a good or a bad thing. He turned to face her. His pale irises swum on a yellow film. "I have no family."

"I have a son and a daughter."

"You are proud of them."

"Yes."

An awkward silence fell. Liss reached into a pocket to retrieve her wallet. She thumbed it open to reveal facing pictures of Hannah and Rory. Dr Edberg surveyed the photos dispassionately.

He said nothing. For a moment, Liss was struck by the thought that he had fallen asleep with his eyes still open.

A low coffee table sat beside the bath chair, as if the chair and its occupant were as permanent as any other item of furniture. Opened newspapers lay in a loose fan. Liss scanned the headlines.

"I see that you've been following the news," she said. "The Martian. The crab."

For the first time, Dr Edberg became animated. His right hand reached out to the stack of newspapers, shuffling them lightly as one might pet a dog.

"It is a tremendous discovery."

Liss paused, choosing her words. "And you read about the circumstances? This is difficult. I'm referring to the robot, Ai855. You were the original template for its brain patterns, is that correct?"

Dr Edberg gave a single nod in answer to both questions. His confidence likely stemmed from the assurances he'd been given in exchange for granting this interview.

"Sir, you may not know me," Liss said. "I'm a specialist of sorts myself. I'm interested in the behaviour of the aye-ayes."

The old man watched her waving hands.

"What I wanted to ask you," she continued, "Was whether you could suggest any reason why Ai855 could allow, or rather cause, the death of a young girl?"

With difficulty, Dr Edberg raised both hands. His thin fingers steepled, a tiny model of the tower in which he lived.

"Life," he said. "The robots must protect life."

A chill ran through Liss's body. "And by life you mean—"

The old man turned away.

"It is a tremendous discovery."

Tim Major lives in York. His SF novel *Snakeskins* will be published by Titan Books in 2019; other forthcoming books include a YA novel and a short story collection. Tim's short stories have appeared in *Interzone*, *Best of British Science Fiction* with 'Winter in the Vivarium' (first published in *Shoreline of Infinity*) and *Best Horror of the Year*.

www.cosycatastrophes.com

The Beachcomber presents

WELCOME FRIENDS TO YET ANOTHER STROLL ALONG THE SHORELINE OF INFINITY, WONDERS NEVER SEEM TO CEASE ON THIS NEVER-ENDING TIDE OF...

HEY! BEACHCOMBER! I'VE FOUND ONE OF THEM STORY CAPSULES YOU LIKE SO MUCH

Mary Shelleys' FRANKENSTEIN

LET'S SEE... FRANKENSTEIN? NO, NO, NO, THAT'S A HORROR STORY WITH A MONSTER AND ANGRY MOBS AND WHAT NOT

NOT AT ALL, WELL, MAYBE. THAT STUFF'S MOSTLY FROM THE MOVIES AND TELEVISION SHOWS FROM THE 20TH CENTURY

IT'S ACTUALLY BASED UPON THE EMERGING SCIENCES OF THE EARLY 19TH CENTURY WITH A BIT OF "WHAT IF?" STORY TELLING THROWN IN FOR FUN

REALLY?

YUP! SURE... WHY NOT?

WELL... WRITTEN BY MARY SHELLEY IN 1818 IT STARTS WITH AN EXPLORER, ROBERT WALTON, TRAVERSING THE ARCTIC OCEAN WHERE THEY DISCOVER A WRETCHED FIGURE HALF FROZEN AND NEAR DEATH UPON A PASSING ICE FLOW

GO ON

THE CREW QUICKLY HUDDLE THE MAN ON BOARD AND SET ABOUT GETTING SOME LIFE BACK INTO HIM

THIS POOR SOUL TURNS OUT TO BE NONE OTHER THAN VICTOR FRANKENSTEIN. HE BEGINS TO RECOUNT HIS TRAGIC TALE TO ROBERT, WHOM IN TURN DRAUGHTS IT AS A LETTER TO HIS SISTER BACK HOME IN ENGLAND

VICTOR STARTS WITH HIS UPBRINGING IN GENEVA WITH HIS PARENTS AND BROTHERS AND HIS ADOPTED SISTER ELIZABETH

WHILE BOTH VICTOR AND ELIZABETH WERE FASCINATED BY NATURE, VICTOR'S INTERESTS LAY IN THE HOW? AND WHY? RATHER THAN THE BEAUTY AND SERENITY WHICH ELIZABETH SOUGHT

AS VICTOR GREW, AS DID HIS LOVE FOR SCIENCE, BUT ONLY MARGINALLY MORE THAN HIS LOVE FOR ELIZABETH. HE LEFT FOR UNIVERSITY TO FURTHER HIS STUDIES AT WHICH POINT HIS MOTHER AND ELIZABETH WERE STRUCK WITH THE SCARLET FEVER

ELIZABETH, HIS CHILDHOOD SWEET HEART MANAGES TO PULL THROUGH... HIS MOTHER... I'M AFRAID, PASSED AWAY

AWW

. . .

AWW

VICTOR IMMERSED HIMSELF IN HIS STUDIES

HE QUICKLY CONVINCES HIMSELF THAT HE CAN CREATE LIFE AND SETS ABOUT GATHERING BODY PARTS FROM VARIOUS UNDISCLOSED LOCATIONS

LOCKED AWAY FROM SOCIETY HE ARDUOUSLY ASSEMBLED HIS CREATION

ABN

BUT TRY AS HE MIGHT HE COULD NOT CONJURE THE SPARK THAT WOULD SEE HIS CREATURE LIVE. DEJECTED HE CALLS IT A NIGHT AND GOES TO BED

VICTOR AWOKE TO DISCOVER HIS CREATION, IN ALL ITS' BEAUTY, TOWERING ABOVE HIM, NEAR EIGHT FEET TALL, WITH...

WAIT... WAIT, WAIT, WAIT...

EIGHT FEET TALL? THE AVERAGE HEIGHT BACK THEN WAS ABOUT FIVE FEET SIX. WHERE ON EARTH WAS HE GETTING THESE GOLIATH CADAVERS WITH WHICH TO STITCH TOGETHER ONE BODY? AND BEAUTIFUL? REALLY?

WELL, THE CREATION WAS CERTAINLY MONSTROUS IN PROPORTION, BUT IT'S KINDA GLOSSED OVER WHERE THE PARTS ACTUALLY CAME FROM AND HOW THEY WERE STITCHED TOGETHER. I DUNNO... MAYBE THE HARLEM GLOBE TROTTERS WERE IN TOWN? THEY HELP SCOOBY DOO WITH THIS KINDA STUFF ALL THE TIME. MAYBE THEY GOT UNLUCKY?

ANYHOO... THE HIDEOUS MONSTER THEME IS MORE OF A MOVIE THING SO PEOPLE WOULDN'T GET TOO ATTACHED.

HUH!

IN FACT, THE ONLY FILM I CAN THINK THAT TOUCHED UPON HOW HANDSOME THE CREATURE SHOULD BE WAS THE ROCKY HORROR PICTURE SHOW

THE CREATURES' EYES, HAD AN UNSETTLING UNEARTHLY BEAUTY TO THEM WHICH FILLED VICTOR WITH GUILT AND APPREHENSION ABOUT THE FACT HE WAS PLAYING GOD

FINALLY, STRUCK WITH TERROR, VICTOR FLED HIS ABODE VOWING NEVER TO RETURN

HE WAS LATER FOUND, SOMEWHAT WORSE FOR WEAR, IN A LOCAL TAVERN BY HIS FRIEND HENRY CLERVAL

HENRY RETURNS VICTOR HOME TO FIND THE CREATURE GONE. THINKING VICTOR QUITE MAD HENRY STAYS AND NURSES HIM BACK TO HEALTH

DURING THIS PERIOD WORD ARRIVES OF WILLIAM'S, VICTOR'S YOUNGEST BROTHER, MURDER...

VICTOR AND HENRY RETURNED TO GENEVA AS SOON AS VICTOR WAS FIT ENOUGH TO TRAVEL

VICTOR DISCOVERS THAT IT WAS NOT THE HOUSE KEEPER JUSTINE WHO WAS CONVICTED AND EXECUTED FOR THE CRIME, BUT IN FACT IT WAS HIS CREATION THAT DID THE DEED

VICTOR REALISES HE CANNOT TELL ANYONE OF THIS LEST HE REVEALS THE HORROR OF HIS ACTIONS

AH! SO IT IS A HORROR STORY?

SHUT UP

VICTOR TRACKS DOWN THE CREATURE TO MOUNT MONTANVERT, WHERE IT ASKS VICTOR TO CREATE A MATE LIKE HIMSELF

VICTOR REFUSES, BUT THE CREATURE BIDS VICTOR TO LISTEN TO HIS TALE BEFORE DECIDING

SO THIS IS NOW A STORY WITHIN A STORY, WITHIN A STORY, YES?

WITHIN THIS ONE THAT I'M TELLING

COOL

THE PAIR SETTLE INTO A MOUNTAIN SHACK WHERE THE CREATURE TELLS HIS TALE...

ON HIS TRAVELS HE BIDES WITH THE DE LACEY FAMILY, UNBEKNOWN TO THEM, BY HIDING IN A SHED ATTACHED TO THEIR HUMBLE DWELLING

OVER TIME HE LEARNS TO READ AND WRITE BY OBSERVING THE SCHOOLINGS OF THE DE LACEY CHILDREN

HE LEARNS OF HIS OWN CREATION THROUGH VICTORS' JOURNAL WHICH HE HAS KEPT WITH HIM SINCE THE FIRST NIGHT OF HIS AWAKENING

HE IS EVENTUALLY DISCOVERED AND CHASED OFF. HE COMES TO THE REALISATION THAT IT IS NOT THE FAULT OF THE TINY HUMANS THAT KEEP HAVING TO ENDURE THEIR FEAR AND LOATHING OF HIS GIGANTIC FORM, BUT THE FAULT LIES WITH HIS CREATOR. THE ONE WHO GRANTED HIM LIFE. VICTOR FRANKENSTEIN

VICTOR AGREES TO MAKE A MATE, PARTLY THROUGH FEAR OF THE VENGEANCE THE CREATURE WOULD EXACT UPON HIS FAMILY.

BUT ALSO THE CREATURE PROMISES TO LEAVE EUROPE AND SET UP HOME IN THE JUNGLES OF SOUTH AMERICA OR ON THE PLAINS OF AFRICA

FUN FACT. TOTO SANG A SONG ABOUT IT IN THE MID NINETEEN EIGHTIES

WHAT? THE SONG "AFRICA" IS ABOUT FRANKENSTEIN?

SNORT...! NO!!!

HE, HE, HE...

VICTOR, ACCOMPANIED BY HIS FRIEND HENRY TRAVELS TO EDINBURGH VIA LONDON TO MAKE PREPARATIONS TO HEAD NORTH TO ACCOMMODATIONS IN ORKNEY WHERE VICTOR PLANS TO CREATE A MATE FOR HIS PREVIOUS CREATION

IN A MOMENT OF CONSCIENCE VICTOR REALISES THAT HE CANNOT MORALLY BRING ANOTHER WRETCHED SOUL TO LIFE AND SETS ABOUT DESTROYING HIS WORK AND ALL EVIDENCE THERE OF

UNKNOWN TO VICTOR, THE CREATURE HAS BEEN KEEPING CLOSE TABS ON HIM ON HIS JOURNEY ACROSS EUROPE AND DURING A CONFRONTATION THE CREATURE VOWS REVENGE UPON VICTOR AND ELIZABETHS WEDDING NIGHT

VICTOR AND HENRY MAKE GOOD THEIR ESCAPE BY SEA AND HEAD BACK TO GENEVA

TRAGEDY STRIKES AS THEY ARE BLOWN OFF COURSE AND WASH ASHORE IN IRELAND. HENRY IS DEAD VICTOR STANDS TRIAL FOR HIS MURDER

HOW TERRIBLE

INDEED. HE IS ACQUITTED HASTENS HIS RETURN TO GENEVA HOPING TO BEAT THE BEAST AND MARRY HIS SWEETHEART ELIZABETH

THE WEDDING GOES WITHOUT A HITCH AND AS VICTOR IS BATTENING DOWN THE HATCHES THE CREATURE STEALS INTO THE BEDROOM AND MURDERS ELIZABETH BY STRANGULATION

AND?

AND WHAT?

AND, WHAT HAPPENS NEXT? YOU BUFFOON!!!

UM...

HE BUILDS HIMSELF A SUIT OF SUPER ARMOUR AND SEEKS TO TAKE REVENGE UPON.

WHOA,

WHOA, WHOA WHOA... SUPER SUIT? WHAT?

ERM... YES, NO, WAIT. I MAY BE THINKING OF VICTOR VON DOOM FROM THE FANTASTIC FOUR COMICS

COMICS? REALLY?

HEY! THEY'RE A PERFECTLY LEGITIMATE FORM OF ART AND LITERATURE

BLINK!

NOW IT IS VICTOR'S TURN TO PURSUE HIS CREATION. ACROSS EUROPE INTO RUSSIA AND UP THROUGH THE ARCTIC CIRCLE

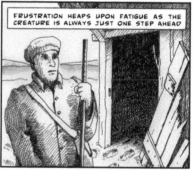

FRUSTRATION HEAPS UPON FATIGUE AS THE CREATURE IS ALWAYS JUST ONE STEP AHEAD

EXHAUSTED AND WORN VICTOR IS EVENTUALLY BROUGHT ABOARD ROBERT WALTON'S SHIP

AND AS VICTOR BREATHS HIS LAST THE CREATURE BOARDS THE SHIP AND TAKES HIS CREATOR AWAY

THE LAST WE SEE OF THE PAIR IS THE FUNERAL PYRE UPON WHICH THE CREATURE PLACED VICTOR DRIFTING OFF INTO THE DISTANCE AS WALTONS' SHIP SAILS AWAY THROUGH THE ICE AND SNOW

QUITE A SAD TALE REALLY?

INDEED. YES, IT SUFFERS FROM POPULAR CULTURE AND FILMS THAT CHERRY PICK ELEMENTS FROM LITERATURE TO USE AND TWIST TO GET WHAT THEY WANT OUT OF THEIR MOVIES AND WHAT NOT

OBVIOUSLY WHEN THE FIRST FILM WAS MADE IT WAS DECIDED TO MAKE THE CREATURE MORE MONSTROUS AND INHUMAN IN FORM SO THAT THEY COULD PORTRAY THE MURDERS THROUGHOUT WITHOUT FEAR OF CONSEQUENCE

FROM THEN ON IN SUBSEQUENT FILMS THE "MONSTER" ASPECT BECAME THE DOMINANT FACTOR RATHER THAN THE POTENTIAL OF SCIENCE

IN FACT THERE'S VERY FEW MOVIES THAT TRULY STICK WITH THE ORIGINAL SCIENCE FICTION SOURCE MATERIAL, MOSTLY DUE TO BUDGET CONSTRAINTS, OR THEY JUST WANT TO DO A BIG "SCI-FI" ACTION ROMP "BASED" UPON THE STORY

SUCH AS?

WELL... WHERE DO I START? PLANET OF THE APES? WAR OF THE WORLDS? THE LAST MAN ON EARTH? DO ANDROIDS DREAM OF ELECTRIC SHEEP, IN FACT NEAR ALL OF PHILIP K DICKS WORK... AND DON'T EVEN START ME ON THE ADAPTATIONS OF EDGAR RICE BOROUGHS...

END

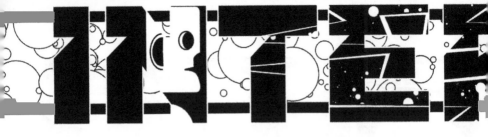

Noel Chidwick: Origamy *is an original and brilliant book. It's my favourite kind of reading, science fiction or otherwise, in that it mixes ideas and story and is difficult to pigeon-hole – as the author, how do you describe* Origamy?

Rachel Armstrong: It's a 'messy' and challenging form of experiment-making that works best when it is unleashed and engaged, rather than controlled and analysed. It reminds me of making mud 'pies' in the back garden as a child. I would start out with some formless stuff and although my mud

didn't actually acquire more form as I handled it, it became increasingly compelling. I seem to have carried this love for amorphous things into my academic work in the discipline of Experimental Architecture. Like *Origamy*, my 'proper' practice sets out to test the limits of convention (and break them), as well as challenge my own capabilities (to the point where I am a novice, not an expert), by drawing together unlikely materials, knowledge areas, media and agents.

Writing *Origamy*, also draws on a penchant I have

Rachel Armstrong

Rachel Armstrong is Professor of Experimental Architecture at the School of Architecture Planning and Landscape, Newcastle University, and has just released her debut novel, *Origamy*.

A former medical doctor she now designs experiments that explore the transition between inert and living matter and considers their implications for life beyond our solar system.

Rachel has long been fascinated by the opportunity science-fiction provides to explore the extremes of human potential and step outside the strictures of current scientific understanding.

developed, in finding ways to make my forward-looking ideas tangible to diverse audiences. An example of this is the idea of 'living buildings' where the materials of our homes and cities are designed, quite literally, to have properties of living things – like growth, movement, sensitivity and even social behaviour. Academia is limiting in terms of how the impact of such technological developments can be conveyed, and what their advent actually means in everyday settings. While being given information about the technical details of these buildings – for example, where a blob of fat in alkali, or protocell, can automatically make a soft structure, and that bacteria can 'compute' – is instructive and says something about the materiality of the encounter, it is not possible to get a sense of the actual experience. Are these things slimy, dry, wet, tucked away in dark corners, decorated with brilliant lights? Do they give you a headache or keep you awake at night? I started to use short narratives to bring to life some of these ideas:

not really as *science* fiction – more, *architecture* fiction.

Further examples are in my book *Soft Living Architecture: An Alternative View of Bio-Informed Practice*, published by Bloomsbury Academic in September 2018, and positions the city of Venice as an 'actor' in a historical and future contexts that inform the design of tools to make 'living' buildings with, through a series of short fiction narratives. This was also true of *Vibrant Architecture: Matter as Co-Designer of Living Structures*, published by DeGruyter, where the dense technical chapters are interspersed with fiction narratives. This slamming together of formats provoked Bruce Sterling to comment on "this monstrous, yet glamorous hybrid of architecture and chemistry" as "cultural sensibility in a gelatin capsule."

NC: Although Origamy *is a collection of short narratives, there is still a story thread linking them together. And characters abound with Mobius' parents 'Newton' and 'Shelley' and her large extended family. What is the challenge for you when weaving together stories, characters and concepts?*

RA: It's a juggling act, where you also invent your own types of clubs, hoops and balls. As these objects are moved around in the juggling rhythm, you learn how to accommodate them, how to make new objects, and learn about them as they join the flow of exchange. Of course, not all pieces are good objects to juggle with, and some additions interrupt the rhythm, but like a circus performer, practice makes perfect and at some point what works for you, persists.

NC: Presumably in writing Origamy, *you've dropped many a club in your early drafts. When you came up with the concept of Mobius and her family of a circus troupe manipulating and tumbling through spacetime, did you have* Cirque du Soleil *more in mind as a model, rather than Billy Smart's circus?*

Contemporary circus was forefront in my thoughts when I began *Origamy*. I'd been introduced to the Circus Arts Research Development 2 conference by Rolf Hughes, who was director of research at Stockholm University of the Arts, where circus artists were exploring what it meant to do research. Without the commercial trappings and signifiers of traditional, or commercial forms of circus, provocative questions arose and were examined in experimental contexts. For example, what are the limits of the performative body, how far can you take a 'trick' for a walk and what does 'composition' mean to a circus arts performer? The explorations were simply compelling. Each provocation raised many questions about how bodies inhabit 'space' – not just architectural space, but all kinds of spaces. From this immersion in a world of weird physicalities and re-configured (social) relationships, which were threaded (precariously) together by trust, *Origamy* was born.

NC: Following on from the living architecture concept, is the organic building programmed by its occupants or some external authority, or is it self-autonomous deciding for itself the needs of the occupants? Where is the control in this system?

RA: 'Living' buildings possess innate agency as they are at least, in part, composed of 'living' things like microorganisms, soils, or tissue cultures. As such, they respond to 'soft' control rather than the 'hard' control, which is typical of machines. They behave best when they have a functional relationship with people. How they behave is intimately connected to the way they are occupied. 'Living' buildings play out our relationship with nature, so when they are abused, they respond in accord with Michael Crichton's provocation that 'life finds a way'. In other words when the living world, in all its forms – dinosaurs or buildings with an inner life – are maliciously exploited, they have the potential to rebel. They may also simply, die. Of course, like houses haunted by malevolent spirits, there is nothing stopping a 'living' building being quintessentially bad, no matter how you treat it. In real terms, we're able to design important aspects of living buildings, so the odds are greatly stacked against bringing something fundamentally evil into the world. Yet 'living' buildings are not 'greenwash', we still have to work at our relationship with them if we are to negotiate a condition of mutual liveability.

NC: Which leads to a fascinating idea where the occupants and the building have literally to learn to live together, mutually adapting for the benefits of each other and for their relationship. Never mind being attached to your smartphone: absorbed into your house. Surely more dystopian, not Utopian? (or is that the science fiction writer in me relishing the conflict?)

RA: The conflict is real ....

It never went away. It's not absent with machines, or any other kind of technology – if we delegate the work we want performed to 'other things' – at some point, they have a say.

Whether that is 'nature', or serfs, or machines, or any other technological construct we use … ultimately we have to build a functional relationship with them. Living buildings are no different but they are a very 'tight' cosmology of how we treat our planet.

And yes, the writer in you sees that …

Living buildings are not a panacea. The answer to better living is that we are much more considerate – all around – of each other as well as the living world. Even then … things will go wrong … I don't go along with the Institute of Humanity stuff where it is possible to eliminate risk. Life itself is a risk. The risk of being alive is death. We have to better negotiate and distribute risk more evenly, as we can engage with it, mitigate, etc. but if we pretend there is no risk to anything, it sneaks up behind us and makes us look very foolish indeed.

NC: *Unfortunately so, as displayed in the near-global heatwave of recent weeks – thanks to our decisions over the last 40 years to ignore the warnings of the dangers of climate change. In* Origamy *we see your vision of a Universe teeming with life, full of wonder and extraordinary ideas of what could be. Although it's not intended as a guidebook for the future, how do you see us*

getting from where we are to where you are in Origamy?

RA: Oh, there's a very quick answer to that: we must learn to Origamy.

Origamy is not a 'how to settle the cosmos' kind of book. It is a hypothetical and greatly expanded portrait of a cosmic ecology, which considers the idiosyncrasies of living things as evolutionary trajectories diverge across the vast distances of the cosmos. It provides an exploratory framework for Konstantin Tsiolkovsky's view that biology is the major stumbling block in settling space, rather than its significant engineering problems, which was something that he knew how to address. *Origamy* supposes that spacetime is not homogenous, where there is uniformity in its behaviour from point to point, but can be deformed, tied in knots and spun out of the very substance of the universe, so the laws of physics and matter can change. This is played out through increasing the inhabitable distances through 'wormholing' that allows Mobius to travel through spacetime. 'Extreme' space then sets the scene for Origamy's extraordinary lifeforms and looks to the 'circus arts' and the mutability of biology rather than machines, to provide the 'magic' of Clarke's dictum, positioning the body and its supporting ecosystems as key to thriving in extreme environments. These extend from the extraordinary capacity of living things to adapt to the most unliveable places, to the changes that bodies undergo, as well as the damage that toxic cultures wreak on the viability of civilisations.

NC: In your TEDx talks (eg https://youtu.be/Vps__XdjZTk) you emit roughly one new idea for a SF story every 30 seconds, and I hope an audience of writers were taking notes. When can the general public come and see and hear you? Do you take your talks 'on the road?'

RA: I hope to come to one of Shoreline of Infinity's events in Edinburgh relatively soon, and March 22-23, 2019, I'm in Hong Kong for the 'Melon' festival, which brings together science fiction writers and scientists: www.melon-x.com. Other than that, I am open to speaking invitations, particularly if there are experimental formats and unconventional challenges involved.

NC: I'll see what we can do! I gather NewCon Press have you signed up for a second book – could you tell us a little bit about it and when will we be able to pick it up?

RA: *Invisible Ecologies* comes out next year. It's a tale set in Venice that follows the story of a boy who knows he's 'different' and his 'twinned' relationship with the land that his people occupy. Their extraordinary adventures reveal invisible dimensions of the historical city and its lagoon.

NC: That's something to look forward to in 2019. Many thanks for talking to Shoreline of Infinity.

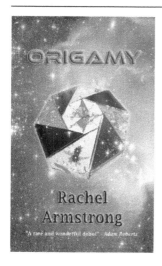

Origamy **is published by NewCon Press.**

With thanks to Rachel Armstrong and Ian Whates of NewCon Press for permission to re-publish the following extracts from *Origamy***.**

Origamy

(Extracts)

Rachel Armstrong

Where Am I Now?

I am still trying to condense, which is harder than you might imagine, as I cannot coordinate my thoughts sufficiently to access a memory or purpose for myself.

Perhaps, if I can foreground my existence with a particular context – rather than making generalisations about the nature of existence in an endless cosmos – my embodied existence may begin to condense around a meaningful form and identity.

I hear my parents, Shelley and Newton, singing of their love for me. I am happy that I know their names, although I still do not know what kind of people they are. Their indelible passion channels my being into 'this' form that becomes contaminated with the seeds of my existence. My conception is sweaty and ugly. While I am not especially grateful for them starting the processes that bring this body to life, the sequence of events that is shaping my genesis fascinates me. At some stage, I may understand the miracle of existence sufficiently to alter my present circumstances – even now.

I attempt to decentre my parents from being the authors of my life and shut out their songs. I hope to establish a purer relationship with the substances from which I am forged. In this manner, I can inhabit this body, 'my way' – not the way of my parents.

I am made up of inconstant forms that arise from twisting, pulsating, undifferentiated landscapes, which the union of gametes have set in motion and are beginning to consolidate through some kind of enfleshing process.

I am witnessing my own embryogenesis – the rolling, pleating, folding and twisting of organic building blocks, marinated in plasma and grown inside a capillary rich bed of tissue that allows my roots to spread like soil – I am becoming alive. I'm made up of excitable fields that spew lively materials and serpentine metabolic networks into a tangle of matter that becomes my flesh.

This vexing condition of existential uncertainty may be choreographed through pulse-like fields, which continually separate and re-condense into structural arrangements that are rich with many potential states of existence. I need to make decisions about who and what I want to be, so that I may shape these constantly contested boundaries – particularly those that operate in the realms between life and death. There is as much metabolism in a decomposing corpse, as in a living body – but the qualities of exchanges in the dead are more diverse. The dead diffuse, while the living, condense. Yet the distinctions between these states create the platforms for those acts that constitute the art of living, where for example, in forming fingers and toes, certain cartilage cells must agree to die. This is no simple matter. Life is its own paradox.

Now, my body fluids seep sideways and upwards as ionic liquids permeate my tissues. In uterine weightlessness they mingle in provocative new ways with their neighbours and begin to reshape my expanding fields of biochemical interaction in concert with the molecular repertoire of my genes. Exploring the conventions of object-boundedness and relative permanence, I begin to establish a particular relationship between 'this' body and 'my' surroundings.

Despite the odds against my existence, I blossom and breathe in a piercing cry – a song of my own. I see my chocolate-red flesh, coated with a cheesy layer of dead cells, for the first time.

Today the world is messy and noisy. The vegetation rustles and shakes in the thin winds. The sod bleeds water. Nacreous algae form oily puddles on the ground and the stones resonate like bells from their bombardment by restless atoms. It is not a day for dying, but a time for incarnation and discovering something new about the cosmos.

But I must hurry if I am to (re)invent myself. These windows of opportunity do not last forever, so I will no longer deliberate and decide where the story of this life – 'my life' – is going.

The Book of Exceptions

You don't read The Book of Exceptions. You feel it.

You might expect a book to be written in some kind of prose but it's not. Exceptions is a manuscript formed by the artificial organs and failed tissue cultures that replaced Maxwell's extracted body parts.

You may wonder how a man who has no innards can actually produce such artefacts.

After his natural innards were eaten by the shade, Maxwell set about replacing them using the latest biotechnologies that reconfigured his anatomy. Although he was stronger and more lithe, he was intensely emotional – more so than ever before.

Finding this extreme sensitivity unbearable, Maxwell removed the first set of innards that he grew using specially designed extraction tools that he'd developed through his mastery of Ancient Egyptian writings. Maxwell used a primitive form of keyhole surgery that left no scars and removed the new innards through his nose. Then he wrapped them between the expanses of organ fat, known as the greater and lesser omenta, and buried them in hot sand. Any cloned tissue cultures that had grown and failed during the development of his synthetic organs were added to the collection of desiccating tissues. He left them to mummify for a lifetime. Finally, Maxwell dug up the hardened organs with their prototypes and bound them in soft linen. He stored them in a wooden chest, assuming that nobody would come across them.

Maxwell was now part of a large circus community full of curious children. It was not long before tiny fingers and wide eyes discovered the desiccated entrails and ran to their parents crying inconsolably. Family members soon realised what these strange fleshy things were and gave them new life and honour by turning them into a book. Then they returned this relic to the chest and buried it in a place where it would never be discovered. By this time, however, word about the compelling emotional potency of Maxwell's desiccated innards was out. Indeed, the enfleshings had already been copied multiple times over and called "The Book of Exceptions". While I can assure you that the originals are safely lost to the living word three simulacra remain. One of these copies is now beneath the Loom, kept safe from the reach of tiny people under Shelley's watchful eye and reprimanding plait-lash.

It is not forbidden to experience The Exceptions.

However, it is advised they should never be encountered by an unprepared mind. To do so is truly an overwhelming experience. Furthermore, should a scholar wish to imbue wisdom from the Exceptions then some skill in divination is mandatory. Various auguries may be used such as haurspicy: the reading of animal entrails, hepatoscopy: divination with livers, scapulimancy: information from the shoulder blades of animals, or cardioscopy: auguries of the heart. Readers of these organ systems do not encounter facts, but wisdom conferred by feelings – a waterfall of tactile poetry with the potential to drive the unaware quite senseless.

I'm in hiding here under the Loom in this tiny dark space as I've just encountered the Exceptions for the very first time.

I thought I was prepared but I'm utterly traumatised by the depths of Maxwell's grotesque abjection. I'm equally ecstatic through the encounter of his sublime resurrection. I'm all at odds with myself and the world and really not sure what I think or feel about anything right now.

While I am no auger, I feel that in encountering The Exceptions, I have touched the very substance of humanity. Perhaps I have come a little closer to an understanding of it – that to live is a paradox – in that we are bedevilled with extraordinary vulnerability and strength. We experiment with these contradictory states through our bodies in ways that can't be fixed, solved, or meaningfully concluded – but through which we are compelled to feel and live.

Fossil Time Twist

We pass a honeycomb planet which resembles a pig's skull with two colossal tusks curling upwards from the South Polar Region.

Two elderly women are knitting together with chopsticks on a rocky cavity positioned on the giant boulder, as an orbit. Their roll of yarn completely fills the hollow and their weave drops as a continuous ladder of highly patterned tears billowing into the abyss. One of them starts banging on the roof of the incomplete orbital bar with her walking stick, because the old couple upstairs, are trying for a baby. Down towards the maxilla someone's straining loudly on the toilet. The whole skull is snoring.

One of the weavers catches sight of us, waves furiously and makes a run for it. Hurling herself upwards over the frontal bone on to the North Pole of the planet, she clambers upwards to the tip of the parietal crest, where she stands on top of the bone-world, her arms flailing, signalling distress.

"We can't help her", says Stokes, "It's a fossil time twist. There's no escape".

As we pass, the woman recklessly hurls herself towards us like a skydiver. She doesn't quite reach us, and plummets down past the zygomatic arch searching for footing on the ladder of tears. She's shouting something. My heart sinks as she's swallowed into the void and I look at Stokes who nudges my ribs sharply and points again at the orbit, where two elderly women are knitting together with chopsticks.

Dark Matters
new sci-fi poems

RUSSELL JONES

Dark Matters

new sci-fi poetry

by **Russell Jones**

Includes

a love poem from Doctor Who to a Dalek

robotic space-exploring bees

a Judge Dredd villanelle

alien lizard teleportation romps

post-nuclear geriatrics

& more

£5 from www.Tapsalteerie.co.uk

Preston Grassmann

Or, the philanthropical beauty of second-hand book shops in Glasgow's Merchant City.

Chris Kelso

Preston Grassmann is something of a journeyman. As a child he travelled widely through Mexico and Central America with his family. He is a Californian of Scottish-German extraction and now resides in Tokyo, Japan. The story goes that when he was twelve years old, he saw an exhibition called *Surrealism Unlimited*, which he credits as a formative influence on his writing.

I first came across Preston Grassmann in 2012 when Hal Duncan and I were soliciting stories for *Caledonia Dreamin'- Strange Fiction of Scottish Descent*. The central aspiration of the anthology was to highlight a commonly overlooked aspect of Scottish society – namely, the deep-running roots of multiculturalism and the influence of our far-reaching émigré. Both factors have had significant bearing on the nations arts. Science fiction being one of them. There are innumerable writers out there working in the field of SF – not necessarily first-generation Scots, but writers with more distant connections to the mother country (but whose work remains intrinsically, undeniably 'Scottish').

Hal was aware of a freelance writer, an American, working as a columnist for Locus Magazine and had been impressed by his work – plus, despite this writer's mixed-blood, he still identified as Scottish. Hal wasn't wrong either (is he ever wrong?).

'The Bouk Puppet Show' arrived in my inbox with a prelude from Hal:

*"This a firm **yes** from me. I say it goes in. Even if you disagree*

– and I don't see how you could disagree –well, I still say this goes in."

Sure enough, the story was fantastic. I was impressed by the skillful prose and there was a fine blend of macabre horror thrown in for good measure. This was true 'weird fiction' – disorientating, dreamy, metaphysical.

The Surreal Unlimited

But I soon discovered this is par for the course when it comes to Grassmann.

His first published science fiction story, 'Cael's Continuum' appeared in Bull Spec in 2011 and was nominated for Tor's Readers' Choice Award. This is a really great little piece. While Grassmann makes his living as an academic (and this is apparent in his surgically-precise-eye for detail), these abstract sensibilities are complemented by his intricate emotional core. In 'Cael's Continuum', Grassmann offers us a beautifully written meditation on a boy's longing for his twin. There is still an underlying surrealism, but it's human in its analysis. I defy anyone to read it and remain unmoved.

There are other stories that simply must be read. 'Broken Maps of the Sea', first published in Nature, is another example of Grassmann's expert balance of scientific concept and emotional resonance. This time the narrative nucleus takes its cues from a theory proposed by biologists Stephen J. Gould and Niles Eldredge in 1972 called 'punctuated equilibrium' and show that Grassmann's preoccupations extend to an intimate understanding of mythology and Japanese culture.

Since *Caledonia Dreamin'* came out in 2012, Preston and I have even collaborated a few times – most recently on an article for Locus magazine's *Cosmic Village* column about defunct Scottish SF journals.

Preston's fiction has been featured widely in professional publications – in *Nature* Magazine and recently in *Futures 2* (Tor Publishing), *Mythic Delirium, Daily Science Fiction, Apex,* and *Black Room Manuscripts* – but his non-fiction is just as dazzling. His nomadic lifestyle has played a big part in informing this side of his work. A career in SF seemed like kismet.

Educated at U.C. Berkeley, Grassmann once lived on the same block as Philip K. Dick. In 2003, he visited the home of renowned writer Arthur C. Clarke in Sri Lanka and continued a correspondence which became a source of inspiration for his essays on science fiction and his short-stories.

In his free time, he enjoys writing, hiking in the forests of Japan, painting, and performing at live events throughout Tokyo.

'The Silk Tower of Beijing' is a short tribute to Ian M. Banks. It's quite different from anything in Banks' Culture stories, but the gun-model reference comes from his short story – "A Gift from the Culture". The Silk Tower relates to The Silk Road, for example, and the delusional hope it represented. This is a glimpse of that world, and an example of one great writer's homage to another great writer.

References

https://www.facebook.com/preston.grassmann

https://twitter.com/prestongrassman?lang=en

http://www.isfdb.org/cgi-bin/ea.cgi?31329

https://www.amazon.co.uk/Preston-Grassmann/e/B00LY0NEYO

https://locusmag.com/2011/05/preston-grassmann/

https://www.nature.com/articles/523122a

Chris Kelso: *Hi Preston. So, what are the advantages of being a writer on the road? I think of Kerouac hitting the open road, extracting what he can from the journey, and transferring experience into art.*

Preston Grassmann: As Mark Twain used to say, travel is fatal to prejudice, bigotry, and narrow-mindedness. I never realized how true this was until I left home. I've lived in Egypt, Vietnam, and Japan, among other countries, and each experience has been humbling in many ways, with new perspectives and ideas that have forced me to reexamine my own limited view of the world. I suppose a lot of my stories are about estrangement, of coming to terms with a seismic shift in one's environment. Exploring a new city, a different culture or community, has certainly helped me understand what that experience is like. On the other side of the argument, there are writers like Alan Moore and Iain Sinclair who have deep roots in specific landscapes and write about similar themes in subtle and fiercely imaginative ways. I think both ways are possible and it depends on the individual.

CK: And what is your connection with Scotland? You have Scottish blood on both sides, right?

PG: I do, but aside from family roots in Auld Reekie, I've always felt a sense of being at home in Scotland. The great collisions of modernity and history, the vibrant culture, the art and architecture – it's all a large part of what inspires my own work. Scottish writers and artists have always been a source of inspiration as well: Ian McQue, Ian M. Banks, Alasdair Gray, David Lindsay, Hal Duncan, and the fierce energy of your own writing.

And not to forget the 12 year old Glen Garioch, which sits next to me at the table, offering its own arcane influences and inspirations.

CK: Do you have any plans to release a novel/short story collection?

At the moment, I'm working on a collection of science fiction stories, some of which have been published in the US and the UK, and a secondary world novel called "The Splendor and Misery of Iris and Spine." The scale of the project has become much larger than I anticipated – I have notebooks filled with drawings, detailed maps and character biographies. In terms of how I feel when I'm writing it, the title says it all. It's certainly the most psychedelic and surreal thing I've ever written.

Chris Kelso is an award-winning genre writer, editor, and illustrator from Scotland. His short stories and articles have appeared in publications across the UK, US, and Canada, including *SF Signal, Daily Science Fiction, Dark Discoveries, Sensitive Skin, Antipodean-SF, The Airgonaut, Verbicide* and many more.

The Silk Tower of Beijing

Preston Grassmann

For Iain M. Banks

The old buildings lean against the rails like cold and tired vagrants, lonely occupants of a vanishing city. Above, a flock of drone-birds hover darkly in the sky, searching the remains for raw materials like scavengers

As I walk past a derelict Tiananmen Square, I remember the lines from a revolutionary poet:

> *Perhaps the final hour is come*
> *I have left no testament*
> *Only a pen, for my mother*
> *I am no hero*
> *In an age without heroes*
> *I just want to be a man*

The crosshatched ruins of the Bird's Nest appears in the distance. Once, I thought it resembled a Chinese ceramic bowl more than a nest, but now the walls on one side have collapsed, leaving steel beams exposed like tangles of straw.

There are still signs of stragglers living inside, with canvas tents strung between girders and broken columns, large flags of older occupations rising above them.

It tugs at my memory, thinking of my father and the football games we had seen there together so many years ago. Another life, another world...

I begin to walk in the direction of Qiongdao Island, where the silk tower stands like a sentinel over central Beijing.

The still horizon
Divides the ranks of the living and the dead
I can only choose the sky
I will not kneel on the ground
Allowing the executioners to look tall
The better to obstruct the wind of freedom

I trace the handle of the gun in my pocket; model LPP 91, series two, printed in several locations throughout the city. The gun is also my key into the living heart of the tower. I think of the old Greek story of the Trojan horse. There are plenty of Chinese versions taught in school, but none of them are as monumental as the one I'm undertaking now.

A lifetime ago, I had been one of the first to receive the signal, an anomalous series of pulsations from a distant star that lasted for 78 seconds. The AI vetting system at CNSA had registered the signal as a false positive. The pulsation, it claimed, was nothing more than the hydrogen gas of comets released in that region of space. Even then, I had known it was a lie. The initial form of the signal had been quantum in nature, designed to vanish as soon as it appeared. Of course, in an age when silicon was thought to be infallible, and with no evidence to prove otherwise, my superiors at CNSA assumed I was misguided.

It didn't take long for the new laws to form, requirements of visual "augmentations" that left most of the city blind to the quiet occupation. It wasn't only in Beijing. There were towers in Tokyo and Moscow, in Berlin and New York, until most of the world had been living in a false reality, designed by the collaborators of a slow but deadly colonization. And I had seen it all, witnessing the fall of friends and family, the failure of institutions and governments. Even the holdouts eventually succumbed to the new technologies, their perceptions edited in a virtual world that wasn't their own.

I begin to pass into the residential districts, where only a few signs of the older world still remain, the bare foundations of living spaces rising out of the earth like prehistoric bones. My own ground-floor apartment is laid bare now, its foundations exposed like a rib-cage left behind by scavengers.

I know it's only a trick of memory, but I can still smell the perfume of my mother's passage, hear her voice in the shadows of the building. I can almost hear her calling me inside for dinner, Chen, Qing ni jinlai, Chen. And the rage comes again, the pain of all that has been lost.

Closer to the tower, I walk through occupied Beijing, passing the sloughed off skin of molting structures and biomechanical buildings. Sometimes, I can hear them breathing, ingesting raw materials, or stretching their foundations as they grow. An old man, modified with skin-grafts and machinery that bulges from his body, vanishes behind a doorway, the walls folding around him. I try to focus on the sound of other trains, the whir of distant machines, but I hear his screams somewhere inside.

I take out the gun and look through its modified sights. Through its crosshairs, I can see the planned architectures of the new city, the blue-prints for a place that will soon become real. The virtual buildings are alien structures laid out between the corridors of a spiral maze. Here, the real structures are all living things, consuming and growing, their bio-fires pulsing through windows.

I walk through the virt-space maze, careful not to touch the walls. Only those with the access codes can see it and move through its corridors.

At the terminus, pipes trail from the base of the tower, the entangled guts of alien industry pumping out materials for the buildings around it. Strange machines grow between the pipes, attached to the tower by thick, body-sized arteries. I follow them around, until I come to vast, pulsing rails that gleam with new ecologies, machines and organisms that borrow heat from the rails and the passage of the trains.

Just in time, I can hear it coming, a train approaching along the rails.

The walls of the tower begin to fold back like liquid origami. There is only a narrow space between the wall and the train, but I move swiftly toward it, following the edge of the outer wall inside. As the train rushes by me, I stare through the sights and take aim, waiting for the field anchors to take hold. I fire it at the train, as if everything I've held inside is finally pouring out of me, blinding lines of hatred and rage. An instant later, sections of the train spill off the rails in a cloud of vapor, crashing through the tower like a tidal wave.

I stumble through its bubbling remains, thinking of Fei Hung and Yin Yue, and Hui Yin. Alerts echo through the space. Creatures emerge from the tower walls, forming out of its substance, approaching with the efficiency of killer cells.

Before they reach me, I fire again, focusing the bristling tongues of power out beyond the veins and arteries of those shifting walls.

The vertical cables and bridges burst, pumping with fluids that spill down like hot rain. Waves of plasma heat surge through the tower and I pull back and run, make my way out beyond the falling ruins of the world.

As a large piece of a structure high above me breaks away, I'm filled with the certainty that the silk tower is an umbilicus, feeding something that will soon die in free-fall or in the vacuum of space.

Their deaths will not be edited out of existence.

People will wake and see the world as it truly is, and return to their old homes and rebuild.

As I think of the world as I want to be, I remember the final line of that Bei Dao poem:

From star-like bullet-holes shall flow
A blood-red dawn

Improbable Botany
Gary Dalkin (ed)
Wayward London
605 pages
Review by Katy Lennon

Improbable Botany, edited by *Shoreline*'s own Gary Dalkin and published by Wayward London, shows immediately it is not taking its botanical theme lightly. It is integral to the collection; opening with an introduction showcasing the tangible effects Wayward have continually had on a world not always sympathetic to the plight of plant life. Engaging with local communities and stimulating communal growth seem to be at the centre of Wayward's ethos. This shines through in the eclectic collection of stories; as well as their desire to put the people behind them in the forefront, with a series of contributor interviews closing the collection.

The collection is made up of diverse range of contributors, from established SF cornerstone Ken MacLeod, to Experimental Architecture Professor Rachel Armstrong. The stories in it are just as varied, with everything from a Sherlock Holmes story to action-packed international escapades.

Stories like 'Strange Fruit' by Justina Robson take a weirder look at the theme; blending surreal horror imagery with hard science.

What investigators believe to be corpses turn out to be beautiful, bruised, women-shaped fruits, being harvested for unknown causes. A botanical specialist is brought in to perform an 'autopsy' on one. There a distinct mood of ominous dread, and Robson's writing is steeped with a kind of lyrical unease, a discomforting depiction of our limited human understanding of nature.

'Who Lived in a Tree' by Tricia Sullivan depicts a more ambiguous picture of the objectives of plants; an apathetic ancient being resisting consumption into the advanced technology of the future. A great tree system called the Green controls almost all aspects of human life; smart-houses are housed within great oaks, and the story is told by a tree living off the Green grid, as a woman threatened with being housed in one of the elderly care smart houses attempts to live in it. Tender, and at the same time seemingly permeated with the indifference of nature, it is a sweet and wistful look at a world where plants and humans could, passively or peacefully, live alongside each other.

'Advent' by James Kennedy is a heartbreaking look at grief and guilt; as the child protagonist grapples with his father's recent death. Plants in the story represent the ultimate unknown. Esoteric, Wicker Man symbology of wheat dollies and sentient Christmas trees, mixed with memories and dreams, cloud the boundaries between real, imagined and dreamed realities. The world and the characters in it are all unknowable throughout the story, and the reader is allowed to slowly piece together fragments from a child's understanding. The terrors in the story are made even more unnerving in their mystery, as though we are being exposed to something far beyond our understanding.

Science Fiction is often seen as an attempt to make sense of our own world and its future. The marrying of science fiction with the vast, impenetrable world of plants was always going to make for an interesting collection, depicting, as outlined in the Introduction, a 'body of work with narrative environments'. The worlds of these stories feel real and conscious. Sometimes passively observing, nihilistic in their disinterest in humanity, sometimes aggressively defending themselves. Sometimes they take an interest, leaning in to change things, for better or worse.

Learning How to Drown
Cat Hellisen
NewCon Press
185 pages
Review by Samantha Dolan

Learning How to Drown is an arresting title. On the front cover, Hellisen is described as one of the most accomplished writers of African SFF' by Geoff Ryman and that might provide an insight for some but it did nothing to adjust my expectations. It did pique my curiosity though, what does African SFF look like?

The answer to that begins from page one, with a beautiful introduction into our author and the circumstances that influenced her. She describes her stories as tasting of 'iodine and salt water' and the duality of living in Apartheid South Africa. When we begin with *The Girls who go Below*, the lake I conjure in my mind isn't the blue/green of Cumbria. The mud is red and clay-like and dense. And it oozes in a way that doesn't happen this far north of the equator. I might not understand what iodine tastes like, but the world Hellisen builds smells of ground heat, of sea scents and people. Would I have felt the same if the 'African' nature of her writing wasn't front and centre? Absolutely. But I'll come back to that later.

In *Serein*, the lesson of the title finally pays of in a very frank way. But where the first story is literally water driven, this one has all the feeling of pressure and feeling emotionally underwater. Have you ever read *Kafka on the Shore*

Learning
How To Drown

"One of the most accomplished writers of African SF." Geoff Ryman

CAT HELLISEN

and wondered what happened the morning after he disappeared? *Serein* reads like Hellisen had exactly the same thought and used it to provide a potential answer.

There's also a fire theme that runs through this collection and my favourite is *This is How We Burn*. This, to me, feels like why we write. It's a story that searches for meaning in the meaningless and uses water in yet another way. Many of the stories focus on large or deep bodies of water but here, rain is central, waiting for it, needing it, dreading the day it leaves.

There are two niggles for me. First, the marketing as 'African SFF'. My concern here is that it doesn't do enough justice to her platform because it lumps all of Africa in together. It's a massive continent, with voices from the North, the South, Sub-Saharan, the East and West and South Africa. And yes, there are strands that bind them all together but these are the same strands that bind us all together. I'm not advocating for more segregation but I think it brings even more richness to her stories when you acknowledge exactly where they are coming from,

exactly what is it that influenced her and how her narrative could differ from someone in the West for example. The strength of her writing absolutely stands up without that generic input.

The only other thing is that fact that each story ends with a little explanation from the author. This reads as a lack of confidence in what she has put down on paper. Readers are used to never really knowing an authors motivation and Hellisen doesn't need these little footnotes. If anything, I found them distracting when I had discerned another meaning, to be confronted by a completely different one. I found myself skipping them after the third story and found myself much more lost in the stories in the best of ways as a consequence.

Learning How to Drown is an impressive Science Fiction/ Fantasy collection, that touches on dozens of themes and just the one, all at the same time. It reads like a personal study. If Hellisen were a portrait artist, this would be her impressionist phase perhaps. The angles she uses to interrogate the questions of being 'other' work beautifully and yet the world building is so true to genre, you often wonder how you got there, what could it mean? And you read it again to find out.

The Church of Latter-Day Eugenics
Chris Kelso & Tom Bradley
Journalstone, 102 pages
Review by Steve Ironside

Centuries away, the minstrel steels himself for his audience with the King. Based on what he is going to say, will he survive it?

Meanwhile, amongst *The Church of Latter-Day Eugenics'*

streets of London, Fulton, a hack journalist, is trying to find reality star Bryan Fix, who has gone missing after his stint on *Celebrity Crack Den*. Will he succeed?

How do these events link together? Come with me on a strange and terrible journey…

Fulton is the exemplar of everything that represents the term "tabloid journalist". He's crude and self-effacing with no moral compass, caring for nothing except his own convenience. His intern, Cheryl, is annoying, the world around him is uninteresting, and he's getting to the end of his rope – contemplating taking his own life after getting one last big story.

Things take a turn though when Fix turns up dead, with evidence of ritual sacrifice leading to a cultish offshoot of the Mormons. Fulton & Cheryl find themselves dragged through the desperately grubby underside of London, to confrontations with semi-emasculated cultists, the mind-shattering drug Blue Lotus, and visions of the sky goddess Sheila and her insidious plan to ensure that only the worthy breed the next generation.

How does a nervous minstrel connect to all this? In the courts of medieval Europe, few could speak out against powerful men and get away with it. Minstrels could, and often did. Their satires, or *lampoons*, were licenses to ridicule the powerful and expose their flaws. This novella serves as a modern lampoon, striking at many things; mass-media morality, ineffectual law enforcement, the absurdity of organised religion and the general public's indifference to dangerous extremes of behaviour in the modern world.

Every character we meet

is deliberately a stereotype. O'Donoughie, the world-weary police detective. Susanna, the flirty madame who owns the porn-shop that's a front for the cult. Nicoleaky, the social justice warrior who becomes key to Fulton's investigation – they could have walked into the story from a hundred tales. That's not to say that they aren't well portrayed – each has their own voice and aren't just window dressing – but they *are* there to serve as specific targets for the narrative that Kelso & Bradley seek to weave.

The locations are also suitably archetypal, from the "high-class joint" called *The Pink Martini*, to the porn-shop with the "neither tasteful or excessively clever name" are again, detailed and colourful; again designed to be comfortable, broadly known, lulling you into believing that you understand the lurid world that is being described to you.

And then, Blue Lotus.

After Fulton is exposed to it, his/our world view is stripped away, and the whole world shifts. The effect is akin to drinking three four-shot cappuccinos in quick succession. The story starts to fidget, then new glimpses of the world blurt out, tumbling over themselves faster and faster, rushing towards the now inescapable finale. The court gasps as the minstrel throws shade at the king – waiting to see what happens.

That pace may be the main difficulty I had with this book. You can't dismiss the psychedelic impact of the rhythm of the text and plot twisting around, but it feels like the book should be longer to allow those ideas to play themselves out fully. By satirising almost everything, the narrative becomes dizzying and wearying, as you try to keep up with the many changes in perception. I came away from it with a feeling of vague dissatisfaction, like getting the munchies after smoking a joint.

It's also a book that only really makes sense at the end – at first glance, a lot seemed like "shock tactics". Only on reflection did I see the path that Kelso & Bradley were leading me down; a neat trick to pull off as a writer, provided your reader puts the effort in too.

Finally, if books with strong sexual language and "triggering" overtones are not for you then you'll struggle. But the message is strong, regardless of means of delivery, so consider challenging yourself.

Overall, I'm not sure that I could claim to have enjoyed this book, but I did appreciate it – it's a worthy addition to the tradition of the lampoon. It forces a look at our attitudes and which warrant saving. That I find those thoughts uncomfortable is perhaps the point. If so, then to Messrs. Kelso & Bradley, I tilt my crown. Well played.

Autonomous
Annalee Newitz
Orbit, 291 pages
Review by Rachel Hill

Ursula Le Guin once commented that the works of Margaret Atwood, 'exemplify one of the things science fiction does, which is to extrapolate imaginatively from current trends and events to a near-future that's half prediction, half satire.' (Guardian) This prediction-satire characterises what Annalee Newitz has achieved in her fiction debut *Autonomous*, for which she was nominated for 2017 The Nebula Awards best novel. Perhaps unsurprising for the founder of science and technology blog io9.com, Newitz's novel follows the trajectories of unchecked Big-Pharma, the increasing erosion of workers rights and the advancement of robotics 200 years into the future.

Told with precise language, fast-paced plotting and a diverse cast of characters (including humans, biobots and biohackers), *Autonomous* updates biopunk – a sub-genre dedicated to exploring the implications of biotechnology – with contemporary political conditions. Thus, "the slow-motion disaster of capitalism converting every living thing and idea into property" is a central theme, where hacktivist resistance is pitted against dystopic corporate control.

Autonomous follows a cat-and-mouse narrative which alternates between the patent-pirate Judith Chen, commonly known as 'Jack,' and the recently activated military biobot sent to detain her, Paladin. Jack reverse-engineers cosmetic drugs for the blackmarket, a lucrative side-hustle which subsidises her real passion, the development of free antiviral and gene therapies for those most in need. It is after issuing her pirated copy of the yet to be released performance enhancing drug 'Zacuity' that she becomes the subject of Paladin's pursuit.

Zacuity instantly addicts its

AUTONOMOUS

A NOVEL

ANNALEE NEWITZ

"Autonomous is to biotech and AI what Neuromancer was to the Internet."
—Neal Stephenson

consumers to work, inducing a state of ceaseless, sleepless frenzy, and fabricating an erotically charged satisfaction in completing menial tasks, resulting in consumers compulsively working until they meet an untimely end. This deadly form of worker optimisation increasing aligns human biology with the escalating rate of production enabled by robotics. The treatment of humans within roboticized levels of production is further reinforced through the indenture of both humans and robots.

Mutual indenture diminishes clear delineations between human and robot. A case in point is the indentured human Threezed, whom Jack initially mistakes for a robot and who often identifies more with other indentured robots than he does with humans. As Newitz states in this editions extra interview material, human-bot indenture illustrates that, "whenever there is slavery in any part of a society, it infects all parts of that

society and we are all complicit." The consequences of indenture are further explored through Paladin's emerging identity.

The resonances of Paladin's name, its Latin meaning of 'servant,' crystallizes the historical conceptualisations of robots as made to serve, whilst also making the reader wonder if a robot could operate outside of its programming and be truly *Autonomous*. The question of potential robot autonomy is also staged at the level of Paladin's body.

As a biobot, Paladin incorporates a human brain, which we are repeatedly told is only used for facial recognition. Nevertheless, this brain leads to humans repeatedly gendering and anthropomorphising Paladin throughout the novel. Paladin's human investigative partner Eliasz for example, mistakes Paladin's identity as being generated by this brain, leading him to ask, "isn't it important for you to know who you really are? Why you feel what you do?" This Robocop archetype, of a human brain maintaining its former identity to control a robot body, is a common trope in SF. *Autonomous* satirises this trope, illustrating how humankind's default anthropomorphisations preclude, rather than enhance, our ability to perceive the true difference of another form of being.

Autonomous is an accomplished thriller and sophisticated work which tackles thorny contemporary issues without offering simple solutions. Like the best SF, *Autonomous* uses a futural lens to consider the ethics of emerging technologies, and the treacherous outcomes which arise if (neoliberal) modes of exploitation are left unchallenged.

Apocalypse Nyx
Kameron Hurley
Tachyon, 283 pages
Review by Callum McSorley

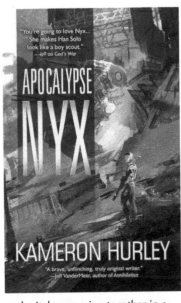

Welcome to the Wild East! The border towns of Nasheen, near the front of a never-ending war with neighbouring Chenja, are lawless places home to smugglers, organ harvesters, and murderers. Nyx, a former soldier and elite government assassin turned renegade bounty hunter, is one of them.

First introduced to us by Kameron Hurley in her *Bel Dame Apocrypha* trilogy, Nyx returns in a new book of collected novellas called *Apocalypse Nyx*. In this series of long short stories we follow her and her team of hardy losers as they scrape a living dangerously, collecting heads for petty cash. Employers are untrustworthy, ill-conceived plans go wrong from the get-go, and violence is usually the answer.

Apocalypse Nyx is a gory, sweary, action-packed adventure that rips along at top speed. Hurley drops the reader straight into her world – a matriarchal, Islam-inspired society where technology is reliant upon bugs and insects with magical properties – without any hand-holding, and the book is all the better for it. There's no info-dumping or awkward exposition – characters don't require things they should already know to be explained to them for the benefit of the reader.

Disorientating at first, the reader is rewarded as they start to piece it all together. It really captures the experience of going to a new place for the first time, where the culture is utterly different from what you're used to.

Hurley's 'bugpunk' is a mish-mash of sci-fi/fantasy subgenres with magic, tech, shapeshifters, and witches coming together in a heady concoction that is mercifully not over-explained. Various insects can heal wounds, fuel trucks, and hack computer systems among other things. There's not much detail on how or why this works and that's probably for the best.

The 'punk' suffix, the go-to tag for almost any new subgenre, is refreshingly relevant here. Whether she's describing a three-way or a firefight, Hurley's prose is blunt, unvarnished, and full of stabbing sentence frags. Anti-hero Nyx is a heavy drinker and nihilist whose unremittingly bleak worldview alienates her from even those people closest to her – a will-they-won't-they relationship with her team's magician Rhys runs through every story but feels doomed. It seems Nyx – an atheist in a deeply religious world – is seeking death rather than redemption.

Charismatic as Nyx is, it's Hurley's world that steals the show. It's a wild west frontier with the aesthetics of the east, all described in visceral detail. Minarets of mosques buried in sand and destroyed in air raids, rise from the ground, bathed in the light of two suns and the multi-coloured bursts of shelling. Along with the air raid sirens are the calls to prayer. Mosques, saloons, and witch's operating theatres are stinking, war-torn, and decrepit.

Hurley takes a twisted glee in gross-out body horror. Putrefied bug-related wounds, rotting corpses, and people cobbled together from parts of others are common sights. Nyx herself has been almost completely rebuilt since fighting in the war.

Nasheen is matriarchal and queer – the majority of its inhabitants are bisexual. All men are sent to the front to fight for most of their lives or until they die, leaving women to run the country.

Men who appear in Nasheen are therefore hated for being deserters and cowards – it was formerly Nyx's job to hunt such men down. There's an interesting role-reversal at play which brings to mind Margaret Atwood's famous quote: "Men are afraid that women will laugh at them. Women are afraid that men will kill them." In Nasheen, the reverse is true:

"...That's when Rhys started to run. He couldn't say why he ran. He was conditioned to it, now. When women in Nasheen went after you, you ran until your legs gave out and your lungs burst." (From 'Crossroads at Jannah'.)

Hurley has fun with this reverse sexism – grown men are still referred to as 'boys' – while making a serious and timely point about equality in our own societies.

Choosing to set out these brand-new Nyx tales as a series of short stories, rather than threading them together as a novel, has its problems, especially if you begin the first story then immediately want to devour the rest of them one after the other, as most readers probably will. Because each one must be able to stand alone, it means going over familiar back story in each piece. Character introductions and descriptions become overly-familiar and repetitive. The same details are picked out time and again – every story at some point alludes to the razor-blades that Nyx hides in her sandals (she never uses them at any point, which seems like wasted seeding) – and you begin to see the formula to the plotting.

Plots usually revolve around a heist which is never quite as simple as it first appears to be and involves a level of violence that shocks everyone except Nyx, earning her the disgust of potential romantic partner Rhys. The longer stories, like 'The Body Project' and 'The Heart is Eaten Last', are the best examples but some of the shorter entries have rushed conclusions that leave the reader unsatisfied.

That said, the pros far outweigh the cons. Joining Nyx's team to get dragged around deserts, acid lakes, and brothels, all the while getting shot at, poisoned, drunk, and verbally abused (by Nyx) is a must on any visit to Nasheen.

Sealed
Naomi Booth
Dead Ink, 150 pages
Review by Marija Smits

For some reason, Dead Ink, Sealed's publisher, billed Naomi Booth's debut novel an 'eco horror' on social media. Put firmly in the literary fiction camp it most likely evaded the eyes of readers who would've been keen to savour this speculative – and dystopian – book, which is a shame really, as it deserves a wide audience. Yes, it is literary fiction, but it is also imaginatively speculative – the main premise being that a new global disease is spreading through an already environmentally stressed Earth, attacking humans and other animal species. The disease is an overgrowth of skin whereby orifices – mouths, ears, eyes, anuses etc. – are being sealed over, causing a horrific death to those unfortunate enough to not receive instant medical attention.

It is into this overheated and toxic world that Booth plunges her protagonist, heavily pregnant Alice, along with her partner Pete, allowing the reader to experience firsthand Alice's worst fears come true.

Always a worrier, Alice's work on the emergency applications within the Department of Housing ensures that her fear of the skin sealing disease – 'cutis' – only increases. She begins to obsessively monitor (and blog about) the spread of the disease, since the majority of the public are unconcerned about the potential epidemic; the media only give sporadic attention to cutis and the more gruesome deaths caused by the disease.

Pete, in contrast, worries about nothing, and is enthusiastic about them leaving the city to spend Alice's maternity leave in the country, surrounded by fresh air and tropical plants. But Alice brings her fears with her and she sees, or thinks she sees, cutis everywhere.

The first half of the book, focused as it is on the characters, (the asymmetry of Alice and Pete's relationship, the exploration of Alice's grief over the death of her mother) certainly bears all the hallmarks of a literary novel. For some readers the pace of the earlier part of the novel may be too slow and the use of present tense an irritation. However, Booth does a great job of portraying Alice's paranoia, as well as her grief, whilst building tension. The last quarter of the book speeds up almost exponentially, and it is to Booth's credit that she makes the finale so compelling without comprising the quality of her writing.

Dystopian fiction may not be for everyone – particularly when current global politics seem frighteningly dystopian – and Booth's overheated and polluted Earth, where everything seems about to go up in flames both literally and metaphorically, is spookily prescient. Sometimes, and particularly as we find ourselves in the middle of a global heatwave, it appears to be more realist than speculative fiction. However, like the best dystopian fiction, Booth allows the reader a glimmer of hope.

Sealed is a hard-to-categorise novel, and it does not make for easy reading. But free of any and all labels, it is still this: a powerful book with a premise that is both original and hard-hitting.

The Freeze-Frame Revolution
Peter Watts
Tachyon Publications, 192 pages
Review by Lucy Powell

How do you outwit a mind that is your own? How do you dupe someone who sees with your eyes, and hears through your ears? How do you outlast someone who never sleeps? These are the questions posed by Peter Watts' newest novel *The Freeze Frame Revolution,* a hard, fast paced sci-fi narrative that really makes you think.

The premise at first is simple. Set aboard a spaceship *Eriophora,* sent from Earth eons ago to punch wormholes through space, this is a ship piloted and managed by a crew whose waking shifts last mere seconds in a timescale that spans millennia. Sunday Ahzmudin is our protagonist, and Watts makes her a compelling one. In fact, despite the hardcore, fast paced sci-fi that is crammed into every other sentence, the story is largely driven by Sunday and her relationships – not only with the other people onboard the ship, but with the ship's main pilot 'Chimp', an A.I tasked with ensuring that the mission is carried out smoothly. Her somewhat complex, and at times heartbreakingly sad, interactions with the A.I, colour our opinion of the ensuing 'revolution' as the novel's plot progresses to make a relatively "simple" mission through space and time, infinitely more intricate.

The 'revolution' part of the novel doesn't happen until halfway through, but the way in which it happens is deftly done. The sense of suspense and claustrophobia created by Watts is amplified thousandfold given the inherently claustrophobia nature of a ship within the infinite expanse of space. Faceless 'gremlin' horrors chasing their every move and the stasis chambers – tongue-in-cheek named 'crypts' by Sunday, where the human's "sleep" until their next work cycle – Watts pushes the pace of this novel into a heart-racing read.

As Sunday struggles to get to grips with both the AI Chimp (whom one cannot help but compare to HAL from *Space Odyssey: 2001*) and follow breadcrumbs left by her fellow rebels, one can feel the net and rebellion tighten. The twists and turns offered as our collective eyes are slowly revealed the truth behind the rebellion, and the

people who lead it, is at times genuinely shocking. Yet, the ultimate climax of the book and the afterword too is one that is nicely straightforward, which is much to Watts' credit. In a book that does much to befuddle the reader – not just through the plot, but through the dense terminology Watts uses – the otherwise interesting narrative is sometimes rather hard to keep up with. This is a novel that concentrates heavily on the "science" part in "science-fiction" and at times, one could be forgiven into thinking they were reading sections from a scientific paper on wormholes written far in the future.

Nevertheless, whilst the novel can be bogged down by jargon – scientific terms that required a thorough read through – this is a science fiction work that capitalises upon an interesting premise, and makes for an engaging read. Although the core plot premise is not new – humanity pitted against the machine – Watts makes an otherwise dense, overly complex novel gripping to the very last page.

Fifty-One
Filles Vertes Publishing, 320 pages
Chris Barnham
Review by Georgina Merry

From the near future to the blitz, Barnham's time travel escapade is a smooth blend of romance, espionage, and intrigue. If you want hard sci-fi, this isn't the book to choose. However, if you love mystery, conspiracies, and vintage settings, look no further.

Time travel is a reality in 2040, and OffTime is in the business of policing the past. In full possession of the Darnell Jump, the only means of time travel, agents are tasked with preventing history-altering interventions, while those higher up safeguard the intel. When senior agent Jake Wesson and his team are sent to stop Churchill's assassination in 1941, it's nothing out of the ordinary. Just a routine jump for a reliable crew. Jake's long-term partner Hannah is an old hand at time travel, as is his best friend Lew, and while Nancy is new to the job, she's already proven herself capable. Soon after their arrival in war-torn London, the group split, and Jake encounters Amy Jenkins. Jake's relationship with Hannah is on the rocks, and his head is quickly turned by the bright young woman. Nevertheless, he continues with his mission and bids Amy farewell. When the group reconvenes, they're puzzled as to how their actions have saved Churchill, but consider their objective achieved. En route to jump home, there's an unexpected air raid, and Jake's separated from the others. Stranded in 1943, he soon realises OffTime have lost track of him.

There's plenty to enjoy in this book, but there are a couple of elements which scream cliché. The tired trope of the older man rejecting his partner for a feisty younger model is the only part that's particularly boring. In fact, it's relied upon as a plot device for creating the primary antagonist. The characters are believable enough, though. While it's obvious Jake is intended to appear complicated and flawed, it's impossible to respect him in light of the way he treats Hannah. Hannah is basic, which is disappointing. Other than moping about and turning spiteful in her actions, there's scant else to her. A woman of her age and intelligence wouldn't be so two-dimensional or

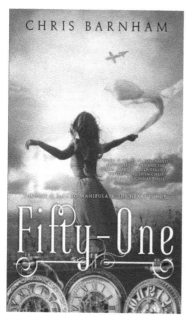

CHRIS BARNHAM

Fifty-One

have such a rudimentary story arc. Even if she was driven by bitterness, why couldn't she be the one to uncover OffTime's secret? Discover what's revealed to Lew in the info dump at the end? The suspense of knowing what was happening through the eyes of the antagonist might have been slightly more exhilarating than the hackneyed fury of a woman scorned. As for the love interest, Amy is portrayed as Hannah's opposite. She's friendly, cheerful, but unremarkable. We're given a pretty girl who, regardless of being the embodiment of the can-do grin-and-bear-it attitude typical of her era, is rarely involved in any action. The romance between her and Jake is sweet and built up over time, but it's difficult to understand what they see in each other.

Lew is probably the most complex character of the bunch, and given how he's positioned in the prologue, it was tempting to root for him in place of Jake. The book opens from Lew's perspective, not Jake's. Then, the resolution is presented entirely again from Lew's point of view. It's a stylistic choice I'm not convinced works, but it's a minor objection in an otherwise stylish tale. The film noir prose and slow-mounting tension are reminiscent of a detective mystery, and the pace is well matched. Tech talk is kept to a minimum but the world-building, past and future, is believable. The depiction of wartime London is authentic and clearly well-researched, and the future-scape is handled with a light touch, using inference instead of descriptions. There were no points when the settings seemed far-fetched.

The plot, on the other hand, had my disbelief suspended on a twenty-foot tightrope by the skin of its teeth. Upon coming across one plot hole shortly after the midpoint, I set aside my quibble in the hope it would be resolved. It wasn't. However, the book ends on a whopper of a temporal paradox that's hard to overcome. If that sort of thing doesn't bother you, then it's all good.

All things considered, Fifty-One is a fun read. In spite of its realistic depiction of wartime London, it is bona fide escapism. It's easy to get through and great for fans of sci-fi genre-blends. What's more, it's perfect for anyone seeking to take a break from the real world.

We don't have room in the magazine to publish all our reviews—visit the website www.shorelineofinfinity.com/reviews/ to read more

125

Beta accumulated

the reach of Cygnus
has his right wing abandoned above my bed
like always, between those heavy sheets
he's oblivious to everything except my fevers
powdery, wrapped by the moon of these dog days

calamity and sweat do not nourish
anyone back to life, ridge-backed sepsis is only written,
they say, in 40 percents on the death certificate
of patients that had died
from this condition, the holes in my moon

have gotten my attention for a long time
with the seven nurses around me
whatever awaits the sick here, I think
under the tropics of Capricorn – influenza,
diseases, broken hearts – will just be another doctor

this one is named Tzum Um Nui on my planet
he is a ruler, a cosmic god
who reigns under my house
for him immense figures with primitive fists
are hewn from the rock

to make me see them
he made the lines visible
when i moved in, brought chalk
into my house located in the former
center of the sun temple

my walls contain astronomical data
and all my rooms are aligned
to the sun and the luminaries

I have jagged plates of stone, like carpets
spread out on the beach
in front of my window

on these stone carpets are signs, embryonic
beings not definable, globes and stars
my doctor warns me
he says the jagged rocks tell
of higher bodies

admittedly, I am not really working
this crimson night, on getting better, I am just in awe
about my cosmic cell
the whole of Cygnus- stomach,
a palace for the sick

and my dog-dreams are bright
in these days, like Sirius appears
to be only because of the proximity
to Beta accumulated plus Zero Three Phi
and its hard to tell the time of a day

because a sickness chooses
double-bound like the book on my nightstand
and the corner-eyed insecurity in between
pages, gravitations constellations and invisible
stars around Beta accumulated plus Zero Three Phi

outside, as the space curls back into itself
I wind also, I turn around too
only to face the firmament of my room
since I know that the number of black matter is bigger
than the number of visible stars

Tris Crest

Tris Crest is a writer currently based in Berlin. She has graduated in cultural
sciences and the study of religion. Her works often refer to the interfaces and
the camouflaging and matrixing of immaterial and material. They talk from the
peculiar perspectives of planets, stars, inanimate things like bird nests or soils. TC
has cooperated with artists and lectured at several performances in the UK
and around Europe. Her works have been published in literary magazines such
as *Das Narr, Rivet-Journal* and *Shoreline of Infinity*.

Skeleton Key

At this instance
my static point is here,
outside my meta-verse,
here in this body,
fluid with matter
lucid and elusive,
pausing in this chair.

Here, my head rotates
round its nucleus
in three dimensions,
cilia reaching for
alien energy dreamt
of when pondering.

While time is running
in its spiral, ever
outward and near.
If I could only
stop drawing that path
aside I could fit this
key into tomorrow.

The heart in this
incarnation has fled,
replaced by a clone
appendage that was
slipped in when
the moon was waxing.

And my sight, well,
it as always envisions
all the aspects of me,
residing where ever
I began a life
living fully and aware.

Charlotte Ozment

Provocation

Inward and out
the spiral runs
too and deep, to
invert the forces
released by that
pinpoint of nucleus.

The fissure is cleared
to birth an alliance,
not yet fused,
not yet realized,
not yet, discharged.

Charlotte Ozment

Charlotte Ozment likes to write about the invisible, the fantastic, anything that would make a body pause and wonder. She lives on several wooded acres in the heart of Texas which are haunted by bipedal, four-legged, multi-winged and slippery critters, all herded daily by the neighborhood cats.
Her work has appeared in many unique publications found round and about, such as *Aphelion, Bindweed, Eternal Haunted Summer, Full of Crow, Gyroscope Review, Quail Bell,* and *Star*Line.*

Cassandra/ Floodland/ Basilisk

After Henri Michaux

1
Because the mechanism/ like a crayon mark on the floor of your
childhood home from when you were small/ because the machinery/
like a shark/ because the color goes out of it briefly when you breathe,
it has to keep on swimming or it will go to sleep/ because the city like
a sickness flutters its gentle eyelids and this machine sounds like that
machine sounds like this machine sounds like all the things some paint
huffing oracle would stay quiet about but look her in the eyes before you
pull the switch

2
Cassandra in Greek mythology was the princess of Troy, given the gift of
foresight by Apollo for her refusing his advances when the sun god came
to her as she slept in his temple and he sent a snake whisper in her ear
the gift of foresight
Snakes and women feature largely in these stories you'll notice
The Monkey's Paw element of this story is that despite what she saw,
she couldn't do anything to change it
She simply had to watch and watch
Unwound, the future ticked inside her like a bomb: disarmament a
moment too far

3
The televised predictions of gamblers indicate the approach of jet
engines, adolescent overtures and other comfortable doomsday-clock
lubricants/ dream if you will, a parched, rusted colossus reaching
backwards through a stream, skin-welded timepiece on its forearm
(unwound and shining)
And this is how we decide who gets bread and who gets water out here,
halfway to miraculous but we ran out of silver to say nothing of wheat/
kicking up silt as its fingers scrabble in the murk: the electric chair is
running on fumes but heaven knows I'm trying my best
If you listen closely to the floor you can hear the clink clink clink like
martini glasses of actuaries counting teeth in the morgues of the
floodlands
So tell me which was it you were expecting?
Some people ask: if we can predict a godlike machine, then do we have
a duty to birth it so that in the future it knows we helped along its

inevitability, so that it doesn't punish us for noncompliance?
That's a thought experiment called Roko's Basilisk, I didn't make it up but my rebuttal to it is this:
If a godlike machine can predict a crash and then avoids the crash, then did the machine predict wrongly?
Here, Cassandra in waiting for her own obliteration playing with a ball of yarn
Everything outside is an encroachment of wildfire unto shadow
Do oracles dream of wooden horses?

4

Here is the transition then, from you eating time to time eating you, grabbing the thing by the tail and having it turn around, what device is it exists outside of time?
The moment flickers like Autumn horses/ candlelight when the power goes out, what a brief silence means to lightning rods the world over
We disintegrate down to flash, like photography, down to light
And the smoke of low odds over algae
I am swimming
Now, here I am: what was once referred to as "poetry for power"
What if an older form of technology could reach back in time?
I'll just leave this right here
And wait and see
I am swimming/ I am reaching
In this/ I am ticking
Because the tender organ like a tiger-shark: cannot stop moving
Toward expectation if necessary or into the deep

Nate Maxson

Nate Maxson is a writer and performance artist. The author of several collections of poetry, he lives in Albuquerque, New Mexico.

"Androids are so old-school," Octobot sneered.

Dane Divine

6 word story

CONER '17

BECOME A PATRON

SHORELINE OF INFINITY HAS A **PATREON** PAGE AT

WWW.PATREON.COM/ SHORELINEOFINFINITY

ON **PATREON**, YOU CAN PLEDGE A MONTHLY PAYMENT FROM **AS LOW AS $1** IN EXCHANGE FOR A **COOL TITLE** AND A **REGULAR REWARD.**

ALL PATRONS GET AN **EARLY DIGITAL ISSUE** OF THE MAGAZINE QUARTERLY AND **EXCLUSIVE ACCESS** TO OUR PATREON MESSAGE FEED AND SOME GET **A LOT MORE.** HOW ABOUT THESE?

POTENT PROTECTOR SPONSORS A STORY EVERY YEAR WITH FULL CREDIT IN THE MAGAZINE WHILE AN **AWESOME AEGIS** SPONSORS AN ILLUSTRATION.

TRUE BELIEVER SPONSORS A **BEACHCOMBER COMIC** AND **MIGHTY MENTOR** SPONSORS A COVER PICTURE.

AND ..... OUR HIGHEST HONOUR ... **SUPREME SENTINEL** SPONSORS A **WHOLE ISSUE** OF SHORELINE OF INFINITY.

ASK **YOUR FAVOURITE BOOK SHOP** TO GET YOU A COPY. WE ARE ON THE **TRADE DISTRIBUTION LISTS.**

OR BUY A COPY **DIRECTLY** FROM OUR **ONLINE SHOP** AT

WWW.SHORELINEOFINFINITY.COM

YOU CAN GET AN **ANNUAL SUBSCRIPTION** THERE TOO.

KINDLE FANS CAN GET SHORELINE FROM THE **AMAZON KINDLE STORE**

Lightning Source UK Ltd.
Milton Keynes UK
UKHW01f0821210918
329231UK00003B/53/P